The Distance Between Us

Marnie Falconer

The Distance Between Us

To those who make my cup runneth over every day, I dedicate this book.

List of Chapters

Marnie Falconer

Lethe

Claudia's Apartment

Pittsburgh, Pennsylvania

Friday, June 11, this year

IT WASN'T THE SOFT knocking that alerted Claudia that someone was at her door. It was a loud, broken sob.

She jumped, splashing a bit of her marinara sauce on the counter. Shifting away from the stovetop and crossing the short distance through her apartment. She eyed the figure through the peephole. The chain squeaked along its track, and the deadbolt offered a small "thud" as Claudia slowly opened the door.

"Eleanor? What are you doing here?"

Her sister sobbed again.

"Can...can I come in?" she whispered. Her mascara had run, and her normally well-coiffed, caramel-highlighted hair was matted against her head.

"I guess," Claudia said, resisting her impulse to sarcastically reply to her sister.

Eleanor stepped through the door and glanced around, eyeing the multiple boxes scattered throughout the apartment.

"I don't think I've ever seen your living space looking so...neat."

Claudia, regretting her decision to check her sarcasm, held her breath and counted silently before replying, "I'm moving."

"Oh," Eleanor said quietly.

"Eleanor, what is going on? Why are you here? What is the matter? Is it one of the kids? Is it Greg...Mom?"

Eleanor buried her face in her hands. A crumpled tissue fell to the floor unnoticed. She sat with a flourish on Claudia's couch.

"Please don't make me tell you. I'm mortified at myself."

"In that case, I'm going to finish making my dinner. Are you hungry?" She didn't press the issue. Despite not being close to her sister, Claudia knew that whatever had brought Eleanor here couldn't be good. And if it was bad enough for Eleanor to choose Claudia as a safe space, it wouldn't take long for her sister to talk. She walked quickly back into the kitchenette and began stirring the noodles.

She took out another pot and poured an open can of sauce into it. Humming the *Jeopardy!* theme to herself, Claudia took a second plate from a box labeled KITCHEN.

From a nearby box, she pulled out another fork and a butter knife. She poured more wine into a glass and took a long sip of the rich, deep red Cabernet. She knew better than to ask if her sister would like a glass.

In the living room area, Eleanor groaned.

"I suppose," she started, rising from the couch and crossing over to the barstool facing the stovetop, "I should start at the beginning."

"You think?" Claudia answered sarcastically, immediately regretting it when Eleanor mewed softly like a wounded kitten. "Sorry. Please. Start anywhere you want."

"Well," Eleanor began again, "it started a little over a year ago. January, I believe. I was having, well, I guess you would call them panic attacks, but I didn't know that at the time. I thought there was something wrong with my heart. So, I went to the doctor. Daddy's doctor's practice. I ended up running into Dr. Nicklaus Scott."

Claudia, who had been finishing up the spaghetti while Eleanor had been speaking, stopped. She gave her sister a good, hard look and asked, "Nick Scott?"

Eleanor looked down at the tissue she had wrangled into a heart and blushed slightly.

It had all begun so innocently. She honestly hadn't remembered that Nick was working in medicine, least of all that he was a practicing Cardiothoracic Surgeon.

But a year ago she'd walked into a waiting room where a kind-looking woman took her name and insurance information and told her to have a seat. She remembered looking through a stack of magazines before settling on doing nothing at all. Looking down, she noticed the beginnings of a run in her tights, where her engagement ring had caught them while she was maneuvering her car into a parking space. Her stomach turned, and she began to feel self-conscious.

That was when Nick walked into the waiting room.

Her pulse quickened at the sight of him. Her thoughts raced back to high school and the way his lips had tasted on that risky night so long ago. The night that Claudia had broken up with him. The only time Eleanor had kissed anyone besides Greg.

He was talking to the receptionist, who began to point in Eleanor's direction. He turned toward her, smiling encouragingly until he recognized her. His mouth parted in surprise.

Holy hell. That delicious mouth.

Regaining his composure, Nick motioned for her to join them.

"Janet, do you remember a patient named Paul O'Malley? This is his youngest daughter, Eleanor...I'm sorry. I don't remember your married name."

"Kouris," she provided, smiling at the receptionist in slight bewilderment.

"Eleanor Kouris," he finished, studying her. She cocked her chin and looked him straight in the eye as he did.

"You are seeing Dr. Williams?" he questioned. She nodded. "He will be with a patient for a little bit longer, but I'd love to catch up with you. I've got a little break in my schedule, wanna come wait in my office?"

She nodded again. Placing his hand lightly on her back, Nick guided her into his office. Eleanor nearly swooned.

"What a lovely surprise, my little blast from the past," Nick said.

"It's nice to see you, too, Dr. Scott," Eleanor replied. She wasn't sure what to do with her hands - or her purse, for that matter. So, she remained standing just inside the door. Nick gestured toward the couch.

"I realize it's been a few years, but why so formal, Ellie?"

Upon hearing her old nickname, she felt a little more relaxed. She took off her sweater and placed it neatly over her handbag on the corner of the couch.

"We're in a formal setting. Would you prefer that I call you Nicklaus?"

"You can call me Nick like you used to. Or Nicklaus. Whichever you prefer. So, Ellie, how are you? Tell me about your life since I last saw you."

"Well," Eleanor started, "I got married several years ago, gosh, a little over sixteen years ago! I have a wonderful life. A beautiful home with two amazing boys that I get to stay at home with due to my fabulous husband. It's all pretty idyllic."

A knock interrupted the conversation. They both jumped.

"Dr. Scott?" A tall older gentleman with a labcoat, bald head and trim white beard stood in the doorway. He smiled. "I'm told you have my patient."

Nick stood and moved to help Eleanor up off the couch.

"I do! Dr. Williams, this is Eleanor O'Malley. I dated her sister way back in high school. We were just catching up."

Eleanor seethed at the mention of her sister, before catching that he'd made a small slip in saying her maiden name.

"We should grab lunch sometime, " she offered, not daring to hope that he would accept. He turned toward his laptop and studied the calendar app.

"Thursday at noon?" he asked. She tried to hide her surprise and tingle of pleasure. The kids were both in school during the day, and she was sure she could make it work.

"It's a date," she answered.

Shifting her thoughts back to the present, Eleanor buried her head into her arm before looking back up at her sister. Rolling her eyes slightly, she responded with an exasperated, "Yes. That Nick Scott."

"I'm listening," said Claudia, crossing her arms despite holding the wooden spoon covered in tomato sauce.

"I lied to Greg," Eleanor blurted out.

"About seeing Nick?"

"Yes. Well, no, and yes."

"Which is it, Eleanor?" Claudia asked, returning to the semi-cathartic task of dishing out the pasta and sauce.

"Greg knew that I ran into Nick at the doctor's office, and that we'd had lunch once. But all the times after that? He thought I was taking a poetry writing class."

Claudia stopped short, splashing the wine she had been about to sip on the counter.

"Eleanor, it's not that I don't appreciate you confiding in me. I guess I just don't understand why you didn't tell this story to someone back in River Styx. Why drive two hours to show up at my door and share this with me, the sister you can barely tolerate?"

"I don't have anyone else to talk to back home. And, quite frankly, Claudia," she said, her temper starting to flare, "it wasn't you that I drove two hours to see. I drove out here to be with a man who happens to be at a conference that is 5 miles away from my sister's apartment, the man I've spent years fantasizing about and months sneaking around with," she paused dramatically. "I came all this way to screw a man who isn't my husband. Now, hand me a glass of that wine."

Main Street

River Styx, Ohio

Tuesday, March 23, this year

CLAUDIA O'MALLEY HAD ALWAYS said that it would take a miracle or a death to get her to set foot back in River Styx.

Unfortunately, miracles are hard to come by in modern times.

Driving down the main drag of her hometown, she half expected to see the faces of former classmates on the solitary figures of teenagers walking through the neighborhood. Then it occurred to her that some of the teenagers she passed could be the children of those she had known nearly 19 years ago in high school.

No, she hadn't made it back in a while.

The town's only funeral home was located on the opposite end of town from where the highway dropped off. It was a big building built by a Southern family in the 1920's that had wanted to bring the architecture of their roots to the north. White pillars supported a wrap-around porch upon which a dozen or so ancient rocking chairs creaked in the wind.

She had to park across the street in a large gravel lot. Claudia swung her car in and crunched to the back of the lot, passing a maroon minivan whose license plate read 1SWTMOM.

"Of course Eleanor is already here," she muttered. Claudia parked under a weeping willow that faced the Little League ballpark. The funeral home shared the lot with the Pub n' Pie, which locals had always called, simply, the "Pie Hole."

Claudia sat in her car and debated silently. Stuffing her Nikon into her satchel, she quickly opened the car door and turned to leave, stretching her long legs before standing up. Having made up her mind, she snuck into the rear entrance of the Pie Hole.

Passing through the small hallway of art deco prints and coat hooks that led from the parking lot to the bar area, she noted that the building itself hadn't changed much, with the exposed piping and ductwork that most pre-World War II buildings used as decor. The interior, however, was all newly designed. The walls had been painted a dark shade of forest green, and the exposed trim was matte black. Naked retro-style bulbs hung over the tall-backed booths lining the outer walls. The same style hung sporadically over the bar. Each table in the center of the room was lit by an electric votive nestled in cut glass holders. A small stage had been built in the front, opposite the Main Street entrance.

Claudia slid through the dimly lit room, taking the very last seat at the bar. She snuck a quick look at the other patrons. A couple sat in one of the booths, eating designer salads and drinking from red plastic tumblers. An older man sat at the other end of the bar watching a golf game on ESPN Classic and checking his cell phone periodically as he sipped from a coffee cup.

The bartender was washing forks and spoons in the back sink at the bar. His auburn hair was pulled in a low ponytail, and he wore a black shirt that had a white pi symbol with beer froth forming the top. Hearing her set down her bag on the counter, his green eyes traveled to the new customer.

"Are you freaking kidding me?" he laughed. "Claudia Paige O'Malley, where have you been hiding?"

She smiled audaciously before reaching into her satchel and producing a glossy magazine with a large photograph of a polar bear cub playing in the snow and tossed it in his direction. He ambled up to her space, filled a glass with ice, and sprayed sudsy cola into it. He set the glass and a straw in front of her.

"Yours?" he asked while motioning to the magazine.

"Yes. Well, the photo. Not the cub," she replied.

He picked up the magazine and tipped it to see better by the light of a nearby bulb. He whistled softly.

"I saw your spread on Iran in *National Geographic* and a couple more in some other magazines. But I've always wondered how often I see your work and yet never even know it's yours."

"Patrick Michael Horrigan, I had no idea you were such an art connoisseur," she said, smiling. Claudia pointed to the glass. "I'm going to need something a whole lot stronger than that."

Patrick winked and took down a bottle of tequila from the shelving in the corner of the bar. Pouring her a double, he slid it expertly back toward her.

"Hey, I'm sorry about Carl. Your poor mother. I assume that's what brings you back to our little town."

Claudia sighed and sipped thoughtfully on the tequila.

"Yes. He seemed like a nice guy. I didn't know him all that well. They've only been married eight or nine years. I haven't been around."

"I've noticed," he pouted. "The tequila request must mean that you've heard that Ellie will be in attendance."

"Her van is in the parking lot."

"Ahhh," he said, nodding sagely. "In that case, let me get you a refill. On the house."

The back door slammed. Claudia jumped, spilling a little tequila down the front of her black blouse. A tiny Taiwanese-American woman walked behind the bar, two reusable grocery bags over each arm. She set the bags down and turned to Patrick, one hand moving to massage her lower back and the other settling on top of her very pregnant stomach.

"I'm pretty sure that we've discussed the consequences of you saying the words 'on the house' before," the woman started to say before Patrick gestured to Claudia at the bar. The woman squealed with delight and shuffled past the barstools as quickly as she could to hug Claudia.

"Oh my god!" Claudia exclaimed. "Deidre! Look at you. You're even more gorgeous than normal!"

"Shut up," Deidre said, rolling her eyes and slipping her arm around her dear friend's shoulder. "I was so sorry to hear about Carl. If there is anything Patrick or I can do, please don't hesitate to ask. So, how long do we get you?"

"It's fine," Claudia replied, "but thank you. I'm staying at your parents' place for the next couple of nights."

"That explains the text that Mom sent this morning! I had no idea what she meant. You should all know better than to surprise a pregnant woman." She glanced at the clock. "Are you going to the funeral home tonight?"

Claudia followed her friend's gaze to the neon clock. She made a sour face and finished off her glass. Patrick picked it up and made it dance in his hand, mouthing the words, 'Come back for more later.' Deidre hoisted herself up on the bar to reach over in a well-rehearsed move and slapped him on the back of the head. Her large emerald wedding set glinted in the soft light.

"Seriously, though. Please feel free to come back over when you're done. It will make certain people's tongues wag, but I'm making a lobster bisque with petite cheddar biscuits for the special tomorrow. I'll set some aside with your name on it." She sashayed back behind the bar and started to pick up her grocery bags. Patrick anticipated her move and picked them up before she had a chance.

"Please, darling, let me take your things," he said in a playful, sultry manner, giving Claudia a wink. "Claudia, I'll see you later."

Deidre sighed contentedly and grinned at Claudia.

"If I'm not here later, then bring your bisque and biscuits by the house, and we'll talk," she said.

Claudia agreed and gathered up her magazine and her bag. She took out her wallet to pay, but Deidre shoved the money back at her.

"Don't tell Patrick - we have a strict 'no sex on nights when something was on the house' rule."

Claudia laughed as she made her way through the room and out the main door.

She realized her mistake as soon as the door clicked shut behind her. Sitting in one of the rocking chairs on the porch of the funeral home across the street was none other than her sister, Eleanor.

Eleanor clicked her tongue once and rolled her eyes. She stood up and walked down the front porch stairs. Standing on the last step, she waited for Claudia to cross the road. The step and her black heels gave Eleanor just enough height to tower over her sister. She was wearing a beautiful black dress coat over a tasteful long-sleeved black dress with a hem that hit directly at her knee. Claudia looked up at her sister, daring her to make a comment.

"I'm not going to judge you for the alcohol, but really, Claudia. You couldn't have made that stop number two?" she whispered snottily when her sister was in earshot.

"What are you even doing out here, Eleanor?" Claudia asked, without turning around. She paused at the top step.

"Jacob had homework, and Eddy needed to study for a test tomorrow, so Greg took the boys home. I wanted a breath of fresh air. Mom is waiting for you." Eleanor turned on her heel and pushed past Claudia into the funeral home.

Claudia rolled her eyes, steeled up her resolve, and followed her sister in.

Canal Shores Park

Poe City Limits, Ohio

Thursday, April 16, last year

ELLIE'S EYES NEARLY ROLLED back into her head. Her heart quickened, and she licked the runoff from the corner of her mouth.

When Nick had insisted, after the third time of watching her order a salad, that she split a cheeseburger with him, Ellie had protested. But now that she had taken a bite, she was a little pleased that he had ignored her. It had been nearly a decade since she had eaten one.

He held an already-ketchuped fry near her face.

"Fry?" he asked casually, waving it slowly.

Ellie nodded enthusiastically and leaned forward to take a small nibble directly from his fingers. Nick laughed.

"Let's get real crazy and order milkshakes next time," he whispered in her ear.

His closeness, the smell of him mingling with the grilled meat, and his breath on her ear were tantalizing in ways she hadn't ever felt.

The day was gorgeous, one of those warm days that creep into a February full of gloom and cold. They had ordered their food to go and were sitting on a bench in the nearby park, where a courtyard of weeping willows gave them a sense of privacy.

Ellie was facing Nick, the left ankle of her tall brown boots tucked under her right knee. Her tight navy blue skirt was modest enough to show off her shapely figure without giving too much away. Both of their jackets were folded and hanging over the back of the bench.

She and Claudia had been raised in a fairly conservative household, with manners, respect, and obedience being crucial to a godly sense of perfection. Or 'attempted perfection,' Claudia would probably snort. But, armed with this guiding principle, Ellie had entered adulthood with several truths she held dear to her heart: her body was a temple, her virginity must remain intact until her wedding night, her future husband's opinion should always hold more sway than hers, and motherhood would be the ultimate fulfillment of her life.

Ellie had held tight to these tenets for nearly 16 years of marriage.

"You've got a little mustard on your cheek," Nick noted, handing her a napkin. She lowered her eyes, momentarily embarrassed as she wiped at her face. He chuckled and raised his hand to her chin. Using his thumb, he removed the last bit from the corner of her lip. "Sorry. You missed a spot."

She looked into his eyes, and her breath caught. He hadn't removed his knuckles from under her chin, and he used them to pull her lips into his. The surprise kiss caught both of them off guard for a moment before evolving into a frenzied tangle of lips, teeth, and tongues.

Nick backed away first.

"I'm sorry. I...," he started, but Ellie wouldn't let him finish. She pulled him back in, her hands in his hair before moving down his toned back. She hadn't felt this way in years. He groaned, placing one hand on her knee and gripping it for a moment. With his other arm, he pulled her closer.

"Ellie," he murmured into her hair, "are you certain?" She nodded, leaning in to kiss him again.

Wrapped in the smell of him, she felt like a teenager again. Heart racing, hidden from the scrutiny of the public eye, she began to justify this little break from her marriage vows. After all, what harm could these few kisses do now that they had happened? She'd just have to keep it in check from now on.

Nick ran his fingers through her hair, tightened his grip, and gently pulled her head back. His hungry mouth slid down to her neck. She giggled with pleasure as he moved up to her earlobe, taking a small nip before pulling back.

"My god. You are just as electrifying as you were in high school," he said appreciatively. "There'd always been something about your 'good girl' vibe, but now? Eleanor, you are so incredibly sexy now."

Ellie blushed. Secretly confused but pleased at this confession, she hadn't ever seen herself as sexy. It wasn't a word that had entered her lexicon until this moment. The best Greg had ever offered was 'fun' and 'awesome.'

"Oh, hush," she said to him between kisses. "You never paid any attention to me in high school. I was just the 'little sister.'"

"Ellie, if I'm being really honest, I always thought you were amazingly beautiful, smart, and kind. And just as hilariously sarcastic as your sister - when you weren't keeping yourself in check. I enjoyed my time around you. I'm enjoying it now." He chuckled.

"Oh, I bet you are!" she laughed. Feeling brazen, she patted his thigh. He caught her hand and held it there.

"Ellie, I'm being serious. I wasn't sure what to expect when you walked into my office. But I knew I couldn't just send you away. And really, how have your heart-racing episodes been in the last month?"

"I've only had a couple. And it was usually around something to do with my boys."

"That's understandable. You're a good mom. So I'm going with my instincts were right, and you just needed to step outside of your usual patterns." He kissed the hand he still held in his. "I didn't intend for -"

She raised a finger to his lips, interrupting his sentence.

"Shhh. I know. It's okay. It's...well...it can be complicated at home. If I'm being honest."

"Tell me about it?"

Taking a deep breath, Ellie slowly unfolded her life for Nick to see.

The Horrigan Home
River Styx, Ohio
Tuesday, March 23, this year

CLAUDIA PARKED HER CAR along the fence at the farthest edge of the driveway. She threw her keys into her purse and grabbed her takeout bag from the Pie Hole. She walked out to the city sidewalk and took a left, passing the fence and one sleeping house. Though Claudia was staying in the apartment over Deidre's parents' garage, she didn't have far to go to see her friend. Deidre lived two doors down from her parents, with her grandmother's house in the middle.

Deidre was waiting on the steps of her house, wearing a soft purple jacket.

"Mom and Dad went to the movies. I have a key, though, so we can lock your stuff up in the garage apartment if you want."

"Seriously? It's River Styx. I bet we could walk right in your grandma's front door right now. Besides, I'm starving, and this," she held up the bag, "smells delicious."

"Oh, don't worry. You won't go hungry when I'm around. I've even got peanut butter ice cream in the freezer."

"Oh, yum!" Claudia replied.

"And I brought home a new bottle of tequila."

"Even better," stated Claudia. She walked over to her friend and sat down. "How are you feeling?"

"I can't complain," replied Deidre. "It's been a lot better since the first trimester, but I've been getting really tired and winded lately. I suppose there isn't enough room for my lungs to expand since someone else is taking up space." She spoke down to her stomach, poking it gently for comedic effect.

"Well, here is something else to take your breath away," Claudia said, reaching into her bag and pulling out her Nikon. Pressing VIEW, she clicked back through a few of the most recent photos, and finding the series she was looking for, handed the camera over to Deidre.

Deidre looked carefully at the screen. A small smile played on her lips. While waiting for her food, Claudia had snapped off some photos of Patrick at work. There were a few of him washing glasses behind the bar, the naked lamp light making his hair light up like fire. The next few were of him talking to some regular customers from across the bar. His kind eyes were evident, even on the tiny screen.

"I can't believe I got so lucky so early in life," she confided in Claudia.

Claudia smiled. Her father and Patrick's father had been lifelong friends, so she and Patrick had known each other since they were in diapers. They had met Deidre on the first day of kindergarten, and the three of them were always together from that day until high school graduation.

Claudia laughed as a memory surfaced. "Do you remember that time you two broke up for three periods in tenth grade?" she asked Deidre.

"Worst two hours of my life!" Deidre declared, throwing her hands up dramatically.

"And Sarah Marie had this grand scheme to win him over, but before she could enact it, you were already back together," Claudia said, still laughing at the memory of their former classmate's dismayed face in the hallway.

Deidre snorted with laughter. "She was our real estate agent when we bought this place!" She stood, momentarily wrapping her hand around the porch railing to help steady her rise. Claudia stood, too, and gathered her takeout bag and her camera.

"Send those pictures to me, please? I'll put them on the website," Deidre requested, as she turned and entered the house.

"You know, I normally charge for that kind of thing," Claudia teased, following Deidre.

The Horrigan home was a beautiful blend of farmhouse chic and whimsy. Deidre had started collecting cardinals, and their cheerful red pops of color showed up in every room. Claudia sat on a soft, stone-colored armchair. Taking off her shoes, she curled her legs up under herself. Patrick and Deidre's home was one of the few places where she felt completely comfortable and right with the world.

Once nestled in the soft chair, it took a few drowsy minutes before the scent of her biscuits and bisque, still waiting on the nearby coffee table, beckoned to her. Deidre had poured a couple fingers worth of the tequila into a tumbler and sat it with the bottle next to the bag. She had gotten herself a bowl of ice cream and was curled, as much as she could curl anymore, on the couch with a blanket draped over her legs.

"How were the calling hours?"

"Fine," Claudia replied, swirling the amber liquid in her glass. "There were a lot of people there. I'm glad that my mom finds so much support in the community."

She dunked a biscuit into her bisque and took a tiny bite. She rolled her eyes back and groaned in appreciation.

"Jed Marteau was there. Did I ever tell you about the note he wrote me after we had a big make-out session in the back seat of his car in senior year and I wouldn't call him back? He wrote about how he knew that I was a nice girl, he didn't mean to upset me with such a level of intimacy, and what we had been doing wasn't wrong. It was kind of sweet, even if inaccurate."

"Well, you were a nice girl, if a little, dare I say, *wild*," Deidre said, standing up with her empty ice cream bowl. "Decaf? I'm not allowed to have fully leaded anymore."

"Yes, please," replied Claudia.

As her friend stepped out of the room, Claudia couldn't help but think back to that wild year.

Fall of Claudia's Senior Year,

River Styx, Ohio

19-ish years ago

IT HAD STARTED THE night Paul, her father, died. She'd been photographing the first football game of the season with her long-time boyfriend, Nick Scott. It was a championship game, and he had driven home from college in western New York to be there for the weekend.

They had pulled up to her family's home in Nick's red Miata. She could vividly recall the chaotic way the lights of the ambulance had bounced off her house and the sudden drop in her stomach, followed by the cold vacuum of numbness settling in.

Gone.

Her life had felt like a candle, snuffed out by an unexpected draft.

The next few days had been a blur of blackness: black dresses, black hose, black heels, black skies, cold rain, and holding Nick's hand through it all. A buoy, pulling her through the crushing river of formality.

The night of her dad's funeral Nick had made a profound mistake. The empathy that Claudia had been relying upon to get her through the coming weeks evaporated. She had confided in him that she had lost track of her schoolwork. Chastising her for being so irresponsible, Nick had suggested that her father would want her to wake up and go on with her life.

Instantly, a fire had been lit in her belly.

With a low growl, like that of a ferocious animal, she had turned to him. "What did you say?"

"I said wake up. Your father wouldn't want this from you. You're being absurd."

"How dare you. Absurd? Do you think I'm acting irrationally? Is this just some crazy female thing? Is that what you are saying to me?"

"Yes, uh," he caught his mistake and retreated. "No."

"I'm sorry that a daughter dealing with the shock of losing her father seems absurd to you, but I don't understand how standing on a pretense of things being right with the world would be better. Things are not right, nor are they good, nor are they fine. God dammit! Things will not be anywhere close to 'fine' for some time to come, if ever again."

"Don't swear, Claude. It's not becoming."

And just as suddenly as the fire had come, it was out. "I thank you for all that you've done for me over the past few days. I appreciate it. But you need to leave. Get out. Now."

He made a noise in his throat that communicated that, being male, he knew more than her before grabbing his jacket. "I'll call you in the morning."

"No. Do not call me ever again."

Nick had paused at the door, shocked at the coldness in her voice. But he didn't turn around.

Claudia the good girl was gone.

While she could not forgive him for trying to force her out of her state of mourning, the real problem with their relationship was that Claudia had felt like she was going through the motions with Nick. Almost like she had spent the last two years checking off some kind of 'perfect life' checklist. Good grades? Check. Cute and modest clothes? Check. All the right clubs and extracurriculars? Check. Awarded the 'Young Woman of Grace' medal at church? Check. Well-liked, respectable, steady boyfriend? Check, check, check.

But death had opened a chasm in Claudia, one that made her question the direction of her life and everything she was 'supposed to do.' The only way to the other side was down into the dark valley it had created.

She had quit every club the next day. Everything except the yearbook, where she was the photographer.

Her sweater sets, skirts, and church dresses had been packaged up and donated to Goodwill. She bought an old, black leather jacket on her way out.

Every single boy who had looked at her that certain way became a conquest, another notch on her lipstick case. Though Alice was worried about her oldest daughter, she was grieving the loss of her husband. She didn't have enough fight in her to have it out with Claudia.

And so Claudia missed curfew on more than one occasion; usually because she had found a ride to Poe, the closest city, to go to an art gallery. She stopped attending church on Sundays and weekly youth club meetings. Who knew what Eleanor had said about her whereabouts to the others? It didn't matter to Claudia anymore. She continued to work hard in school. She had a new goal - get high-paying scholarships to a West Coast university and leave River Styx behind.

With all of her new free time, Claudia began to develop her passion for photography. She started taking portraits of families in River Styx, pouring any money she made back into learning more about the effects of light and darkness on film.

By the end of her senior year, she had amassed so many pieces that a local gallery gave her the space to have a one-night-only showing of her work. Deidre and Patrick had filched a bottle of champagne from his dad's collection at the Pie Hole, where they both worked on weekends and during the dinner rush, to celebrate.

That night, Claudia's career was born, and she found her way out of the darkness.

The Kouris Home,

River Styx, Ohio

Thursday, March 18, this year

ELLIE HAD TAKEN ADVANTAGE of a program that allowed her to earn college credits while still in high school, and, as a result, had obtained an associate's degree in accounting by the end of her senior year, nearly two years after her father, Paul, had died. That summer, she went to work at a local firm, where she met Gregory Kouris.

Though he was six years older than her, Ellie thought he was handsome, cosmopolitan, and mature. He'd grown up in the home of his Greek grandparents on the East Coast, attended college out west, and had spent 20 months living in Istanbul as a missionary.

Even though it wasn't required of him, he wore a suit and tie to work almost every day. Though modest, the cut worked perfectly for his sculpted thighs and tight butt - a running back's body, Ellie would come to learn. She'd nervously turn her gaze down whenever he'd smile at her, convinced he knew she was thinking about the way the suit fabric slid over his muscles in beautiful ways. His dark-haired, light brown-eyed boy-next-door charm had all the ladies at work smitten. Divorcées would bake him cookies, and mothers would point to pictures on their desks of single daughters away at college, but it was Ellie for whom he had eyes.

And once she'd caught on to that fact, Ellie was not letting him go.

Their first date was dinner at a swanky restaurant and then to see a touring revival of *Wicked* at Playhouse Square. While both had been quiet and shy on the way up to the city, on the way home, they sang the whole score and any other Broadway tunes they could think of at the tops of their lungs. Breathless, giggling, and longing to stay in each other's company, they stopped for dessert at an all-night diner just off the highway - two minty grasshopper sundaes with extra cherries. And to top it all off, he called her beautiful terms of endearment in Greek, which he spoke fluently.

It was a perfect night in Ellie's young eyes.

Greg had the perfect choir boy persona that she'd always imagined herself marrying. Handsome, for sure, but also smart, kind, and devoted. A true Eagle Scout, for what it was worth. He certainly met all of Alice's requirements for her girls.

And he was waiting for marriage to give himself sexually to his eternal partner.

They dated for four months before he whisked her away to his hometown to pop the question with a 1.5-carat ring.

They married that October. She worked at the firm until the third trimester of her first pregnancy, then settled nicely into domestic life and never looked back.

Now, she stood in the naturally-lit stairwell, studying a 16x20 inch framed photo from their wedding day. They were standing, hand in hand, in a field of sunflowers. She'd convinced the photographer, who was decidedly not her sister, to pop out to a couple of fields that morning to gauge which had the best blooms. Ellie had also figured out what time would produce the best angle of the sun. She had put so much energy and work into this one touchstone of their life, just as she did with everything.

For his part, Greg had always been game for anything Ellie wanted. He was completely smitten with his wife, then and now. But maybe that was the problem. They had isolated themselves on their little island, with Ellie believing their vanilla passion was all that life had to offer. She wondered if Greg ever felt the same.

Ellie sighed loudly before wiping the wooden frame with a bit of oil soap, as she did every other Thursday. She continued cleaning down the wall: pictures of her two boys as infants, a shadow box for each of them with their take-home clothes and various baby paraphernalia, annual photos for each boy with a matching family shot - the photographic evidence of a life well planned.

She hadn't intended for things with Nick to get this far. She gave herself a minute to check her phone. Ellie swiped past her messenger app and went straight to the notes section where she'd hidden some of her favorite messages under a Christmas list from four years ago. The latest passage was from last night, where she'd teased Nick that he was falling for her and prodded for an honest answer.

> As in what you said? Yeah, of course, I am falling for you, damn it. That's obvious. Yes, I worry about getting deep in my head with it, but dear god! You have it bad is a good description.

Her heart beat faster, and she scrolled up, looking for the message from last week.

> I just wanted to say that I was thinking about your eyes, and then your lips, and how sweet your lips are…but
>
> that made me think of the first kiss this afternoon.

And now? What had she become? Your stereotypical suburban housewife. Conquer one king in one castle with charm, paint, elbow grease, and a good vision board before it's off to the next!

She laughed at the thought of storming a castle armed with a sword and a TikTok account as she moved into the laundry room to pour out her dirty water. She glanced out the window at the ornamental pear trees lining her drive. The rain was pouring down now, hard enough to bounce off the budding leaves.

She was surprised to find her cheeks wet with tears, mirroring the branches outside.

Mount Hope Cemetery

River Styx, Ohio

Wednesday, March 24, this year

CLAUDIA PULLED HER SCARF up closer to her ears. The wind was bitter and cold as it plowed across the cemetery.

She was standing in between her brother-in-law, Greg, and her mother. As they bowed their heads to pray, Claudia noted Deidre and Patrick in the back of a cluster of people. Most of the people in attendance were people she had known growing up, the vanguard of the close-knit community of River Styx. Before retiring, her stepfather had owned a family-run pharmacy downtown. Many of the mourners were fellow business owners or Rotary buddies and their wives. But a man she didn't know was standing next to Patrick. He was tall with dark hair. His light blue eyes caught hers, and she realized she had been staring.

The funeral director had finished the service and reached over to shake hands with Claudia and her family. Murmuring her appreciation, she excused herself from Alice's side and ventured over to where Deidre was standing.

"Hey," she said as she approached the couple.

Patrick reached over and hugged Claudia. Deidre reached out and squeezed her hand.

"I hate funerals," he whispered to the group, sliding his arm around his wife.

"You and me, both," Claudia replied.

"It's this part," said Deidre, agreeing with her husband. "Do you leave? Do you say, 'I'm sorry for your loss' one more time?"

Claudia looked out across the cemetery to the O'Malley family plot.

"I'm not sure it matters," she declared to the safety net of her old friends. "I don't remember what anyone said or did after Dad's funeral. Time was weird, like it was slow and fast at the same time." She shrugged. Deidre's hand found hers again. She squeezed it gently.

The man she'd noticed earlier was hovering near the group.

"Claudia, I want to introduce you to Spencer Siegel," said Deidre.

"Hi, Spencer. It's nice to meet you," she replied, reaching out her hand. He took it and shook it, a nice firm grip. His hand was warm despite the cold weather.

"Spencer moved in, what? Five or so years ago," Deidre continued, glancing at Spencer for confirmation. "He's running the library."

"Well, I wouldn't say 'running,'" stated Spencer, scrunching up his face. "I think, technically, that I'm the Communications Director." He paused. "I'm really sorry. Carl volunteered at the library every Thursday. He was a wonderful man. We will miss him."

"Thank you," she said and gave him a wistful smile, hoping that her complete ignorance of her stepfather's habits wasn't written plainly across her face.

"It was very nice to meet you, Claudia. Dee, Patrick, I'll see you later?" he said, his eyebrows popping up inquisitively over his ocean-blue eyes.

"I hope so," Deidre laughed. "It's lobster bisque day! I made extra biscuits because I know they're your fav!"

Spencer walked over in the direction of Alice. He shook hands with Greg and gave Eleanor a brief hug. When her mother turned her attention to him, Spencer hugged her and held her hand, obviously offering an extended version of his sympathies. Everyone seemed very familiar with each other, and Claudia began to wonder what else she was missing about her family's lives here at home.

"Claudia!" Deidre half-shouted.

Claudia jumped. "I'm sorry. What were you saying?" she replied.

"I was just asking if you were coming back to the Pie Hole or if you were going to go home to your mother's."

Claudia looked around the cemetery. She had always found it soothing. It had a certain morose charm, the mix of old and new gravestones. It was the oldest burial ground in the county and dated back to the 1810s when River Styx had been founded. The late morning light offered interesting shadows, and she longed to do a still-life study of the statuary.

"I think I'm going to shoot some pictures, then go to my mom's," she replied. "What time are you leaving the restaurant?"

Deidre rubbed her stomach and held a silent conversation with Patrick, in the way that couples who have been together for a long time can. Wrinkling her nose up and down, she finally answered. "Probably six. Come on over to our house when you're done."

The Horrigan Home

River Styx, Ohio

Wednesday, March 24, this year

"I NEED A DRINK."

Deidre surveyed her friend standing in the doorway. Claudia had changed into gray sweatpants and a black long-sleeved t-shirt. Her electric orange Converse stood in stark contrast to the muted tones of the rest of her clothes. She hadn't bothered to put on a coat for the walk over.

"Your wish is my command!" sang Deidre as she produced the highball glass of bourbon barrel tequila she had sat on the end table next to the door. From the slam she'd heard coming from her parents' driveway, she'd known Claudia would be there soon. "I've got a fire going in the backroom. Wanna sit back there?"

Claudia took a swig of her drink. She breathed in to feel the fire of the liquid in her throat. She wrinkled her nose. "You have a back room? I don't remember that."

"We've done a little remodeling in the last ten years," Deidre said, motioning for her friend to follow. They walked through the kitchen and out a set of French sliding doors to a glass-enclosed room. At the far edge of the space was a lovely fire blazing in the dim light.

"Dee! It's gorgeous!" Claudia exclaimed.

"I know! I love this room. Can you just imagine playing Barbies out here?"

Claudia smiled and reached out to her old friend. "You are going to be such a good mom."

Deidre laughed, tears welling up in her eyes. "I'm certainly going to try!"

The two sat down on the couch in front of the fireplace, their arms still wrapped around each other. They did not need words to convey their emotions to each other, and the room settled into a comfortable silence. Claudia sipped on her drink thoughtfully.

She had always known the best places to hide in plain sight at her mother's house and had been sitting in one such place, nibbling on a chunk of ham, when her mother pounced.

"Claudia, what do you think about sitting with Aunt Maureen for a little while?"

Claudia was sure she didn't have an aunt named Maureen and gave her mother a narrowed-eye look of confusion.

"Claudia? Carl's sister. And I'm not giving you a pass on this one," her mother said, and pointed to a woman with wispy, red dyed hair and wearing a plum pantsuit, and sitting on the couch.

While her father had been her guiding light, it was Alice who had bought that first camera for her. The problem with Alice was that she and her oldest daughter were too much alike. Both were confident in their opinion, but while Claudia was tactfully direct, her mother would needle and nag to get her point across.

Alice had aspired to be a painter when she was young. But the romance of young love and duty had gotten in the way. At her own mother's suggestion, she used the money she'd saved up to study in Paris on a modest wedding and a down payment on a four-bedroom house. Eight months later, Claudia was born. Shorn of her Parisian dreams, Alice had named her after the French impressionist painter, Claude Monet. Eleven months after that, Eleanor, named for Élie Anatole Pavi, another impressionist, came along.

If she held it against Claudia's father, it never came across. They were deeply in love.

Well, Claudia thought, *how bad could it be sitting with a stranger talking about another stranger?*

She dropped her plate off on the kitchen counter and made her way to the woman.

"Maureen?" She asked, kneeling next to the woman. "Hi, I'm Claudia. I'm Alice's daughter."

Maureen studied her with red-rimmed eyes. The skin on her pale face was papery and dry.

"Claudia? I thought your name was Eleanor. Oh, no, wait. That's right. Alice has two daughters. How are you holding up, dear?" She leaned back to study the young woman. "Oh! You look just like your mother when she was younger!"

There's one strike against this woman, Claudia thought.

"Did I ever tell you about how I met your mother?" Maureen asked.

Claudia stifled a sigh and settled on the floor at the woman's feet, plastering a kind smile on her face. "No. Please do."

"I worked the fragrance counter and the front register at my daddy's shop, you know, the one Carl ran?"

With a nod, Claudia silently celebrated that she had finally heard a piece of information that she had already known.

"Well," Maureen continued, "Alice would always come in on Wednesdays to buy a new sketchbook. We kept a couple of little artsy things in stock. Crayons, pencils, paper, that kind of stuff. She was the cutest little thing. Almost always had a homemade dress on, but they were beautiful! Just gorgeous, with little bits and bobs and embroidery on them!

"Anyway, I got to know her that way, as one of the regular customers for a couple of years. Until one day, she came in and said, 'Miss Reeni,' everyone called me Reeni back then, 'Miss Reeni, I think that I'd like to purchase some perfume, please.' So we sprayed a couple of scents, and I'll never forget it: she chose Love's Baby Soft. So, I wrapped it up nicely for her.

"A couple of weeks later, she came in for some lipstick. And I knew she was a goner for some boy! And what a nice young man your father was, too! I was so sorry to learn that he'd passed."

She patted Claudia's arm with her thin hand. "Don't you worry, though. Carl was a good man, too. He's taken good care of your mother and your sister."

"He certainly did," came Eleanor's voice from behind. Claudia looked up at her sister.

"Aunt Maureen, do you mind if I steal Claudia for a minute?"

"Not at all, my dear," replied Maureen. "I think I'll have another piece of pie." Claudia stood up, then helped the woman up and steadied her.

"What do you want, Eleanor?" she asked.

"I need your help. Mom wants to clean some things out of the attic, and I can't do it alone. No," she paused and held up a finger. "It's not fair that I have to do it alone. This is your world, too."

"Is it?" Claudia replied. "Barely anything left here is mine."

"And whose fault is that?" Eleanor nearly hissed. "Your own. Now. Are you going to help or not?"

Claudia sighed. "When?"

"Tomorrow. We'll start in the morning."

Canal Shores Parking Lot

Poe City Limits, Ohio

Friday, March 19, this year

THE SOFT RINGTONE ASSIGNED to her mother was going off in her purse. But the chill of his cold fingers was too amazing to ignore.

"Oh my stars," she moaned as Nick's mouth traveled down her neck.

Ellie opted to get off before answering her mother's call.

"Don't stop," she pleaded with Nick. "Please, don't stop!"

Her breath caught and broke as she crested. Nick, clearly pleased with himself, cleared his throat softly. He locked eyes with her and licked the fingers he'd just used to send her over the edge.

Ellie laughed breathlessly and leaned in to kiss his lips.

When she'd known him back in high school, Ellie had thought his dark eyes and lightly muscled physique were the sexiest things about him. But now, she had a whole list. There was the adorable little noise he made when he was turned on by her, the comfortable way his hand reached for her thigh when she sat in the passenger seat of his car, and how he'd confessed that he'd get hard just thinking about the taste of her arousal.

They were sitting, like two teenagers, in the leather and wood-paneled backseat of his BMW SUV, parked in a lesser-used corner of a downtown lot. She pushed her skirt back down and leaned back into his arms, holding one of his hands in hers.

Ellie sighed contentedly.

In just a few weeks, her eyes had been opened to a world that she'd not known existed. Cocooned in her young marriage, with two young children before her 21st birthday, Ellie's entire life had been wrapped narrowly in playdates, school bake sales, parent-teacher association presidency, keeping a beautiful home, and a happy husband. But this fire she felt throughout her was new, a sexual awakening that drove her to justify the unthinkable. She had broken her marriage vows, though she hadn't been the one to let the marital bed go cold. The truth was, she was so filled with concupiscence that it had only taken the faintest movement to send her tumbling over the edge.

For all of her adult experience, she was still so sheltered in her worldview. Nick teased her that she was like a line in that old Adam Ant song - if you don't drink and don't smoke, what do you do?

Well. They had an answer now. Him. She'd do him as long as she could.

Nick was checking emails on his phone with one hand when Ellie bolted upright.

"Mom," she reminded herself and reached for her own phone.

"Oh, that's right," replied Nick, clearly engaged in studying a patient's case file he'd pulled up on the screen.

Ellie tapped the callback button with a pale green nail.

"Ellie," her mother answered the phone with a tone that made it clear she had been crying.

"Hi, Mom," Ellie replied in a concerned voice. Nick glanced at her, but she waved off his concern. "What's going on? Is everything okay?"

"Oh, honey," started Alice, her voice breaking. "It's Carl."

Ellie turned to look at Nick, who had turned his full attention to her. She reached for his hand and slid until her back was against the seat of the car.

"Carl died this morning, honey. Can you come help me with all the arrangements? And can you call Claudia and let her know?"

"Of course. Yes. Of course I can, Mom." After her orgasmic bliss, Ellie's mind was struggling to catch up to the revelation that her stepfather had passed away. She took a small notebook out of her purse and began to make notes: *Arrangements with the funeral home: Greg writes the obituary(?) Flowers. Claudia.* "I'll be over to the house as soon as I can."

"Thank you. I appreciate it."

Ending the call, Ellie turned to look at Nick. She pulled him close and kissed his nose.

Carl had been the only grandfather her children had known, and Ellie was grateful to him for all he had done for her mother in the past nine or so years. But she had already mourned her real father all those years ago. Not to say that she wasn't sad that Carl was gone. But at this moment, it simply wasn't as impactful to her.

"I have something I need to take care of first," she murmured in Nick's ear as she slid her hands to his belt, button, and zipper. She'd been reading about giving mind-blowing blowjobs, and, never having been given a reason to try, she wanted to see if she could send him over the edge as he did with her. With the barrier of his pants breached, Ellie reached for his reawakened cock and teasingly licked at the tip before fully engaging. Nick made a little sound in his throat, and she smiled to herself. She needed to take care of this before facing the real-world scenario that awaited her at her mother's house.

The Horrigan Home
River Styx, Ohio
Wednesday, March 24, this year

DEIDRE AND CLAUDIA WERE both dozing when Patrick stepped into the room.

"Wake up, girls, we've got company," he said.

Spencer was behind him. He seemed familiar with the space as he removed his coat and scarf and laid them over a chair in the corner. He stepped up to Deidre and half-hugged her before taking the bottle of beer that Patrick was offering him. They both sat on the floor, close to the fire but facing the couch.

"I promised Spencer the opportunity to hang out with the artist behind all the photographs at the library," he said, offering a beer to Claudia. She took it, still a little groggy and slightly puzzled.

"What photos at the library?" she said.

"Carl made a media request and donation to the library," explained Spencer. "Nine poster-sized prints of various worldwide treasures, professionally framed and hung up in the reading room. Plus annual subscriptions to *National Geographic, Smithsonian, Life,* and *Reader's Digest.*"

Claudia looked confused.

"I think," Spencer continued, "that he just really liked the *Reader's Digest.*"

He smiled, and Claudia laughed.

"He was proud of you and your work and excited to show it off to all of River Styx."

"Well," Claudia started, blushing from either the liquor she'd consumed earlier, the heat of the fire, or the embarrassment of not knowing one more thing about her stepfather, "that does explain one sizable check from Art.com."

"He was, Claude," said Patrick. "But I think he knew that you didn't have to need him, so he was happy just being your hometown cheerleader."

Claudia sipped her beer and stared into the fire. "I didn't know," she whispered.

Deidre reached over to scratch Claudia's back, then hoisted herself off the couch. "I'm starving. I'll make us some snacks."

Patrick smiled lovingly, watching his wife waddle from the room.

Spencer cleared his throat.

"Patrick was just telling me that you all grew up together," he said. "And that you were always the quiet one."

"Yeah," Claudia agreed. "That's probably true. Patrick and Dee were a force to be reckoned with, and I just sorta tagged along."

"I don't know that I would go that far," said Patrick. "You were as much of an instigator!"

"I was always afraid that we'd be seen and that someone would call and tell my mom! Remember when we went for a bike ride around the middle school, and Mrs. Johnson almost hit me with her car? I was so terrified that she'd stop by the house!" Claudia laughed. "Now, as an adult, I realize that she was probably equally terrified that someone would tell my mom about her!" Claudia continued. "Isn't it funny? Sometimes, I feel like I exist on two planes. There's the me who is still 12 years old and who only knows a narrow sliver of what's going on, and the adult who knows the rest of the story."

"Yes!" Spencer agreed enthusiastically, saluting her with his beer bottle. "I know exactly what you mean."

"I feel that way sometimes when I'm at a historic site," Claudia continued. "I can almost feel the people who have been there over the centuries. So, I photograph the story from their angle. But I also see the wonder of something so old existing in modernity. So I shoot that angle, as well."

"I can see now why your photos are so amazing," Spencer smiled. Claudia was suddenly struck by what a nice smile it was, full lips over adorably crooked front teeth. She found herself wondering what they would taste like and blushed again. She normally wasn't so self-conscious about such thoughts, but the combination of being home with memories of her family and her childhood had made her guarded.

Deidre crept in quietly and placed a tray of crackers, cheese, and Oreos on the end table before folding back into the comfort of the couch.

"You should see the yearbook photos she took. Her talent came through, even then," Deidre said, pulling apart an Oreo before popping one side in her mouth.

Claudia rolled her eyes at Spencer, who smiled.

"Well," Deidre amended, "at the very least, our wedding photos!"

"Tell me about yourself, Spencer," Claudia said, redirecting the conversation.

"Do you want the elevator pitch or the long-form essay?"

They all laughed.

"Whichever."

"Okay," he said, twitching his lips in a way that made Claudia's breath catch, "I grew up in Pittsburgh. Played a little lacrosse and a lot of Dungeons and Dragons. I went to college and got a Bachelor's in English. Worked for a little while at a greeting card company. Then, I went back to do a Master's in Library Science. Decided that big city life was too much for me, I found this job, and here I am. I've met a lot of great people and ate an absurd amount of pie. And that's about it."

"What part of Pittsburgh?" Claudia asked, catching the sly smile between Deidre and Patrick.

"I grew up in Deutschtown, but we moved to Cranberry when I started high school."

"You're kidding. My apartment is in East Allegheny! Right on the river. I'm rarely there, but when I am, I love it. The architecture and shadows are positively gorgeous."

"Yes. It is. But, Miss Big-Time-Photographer, why Pittsburgh?"

"It's too expensive to maintain an apartment that I barely use in New York. Pittsburgh was the closest international airport that wasn't in the same state as my family," Claudia winked and took a sip of her drink. "Plus, the amazing bars and shops of Carson Street."

Spencer laughed.

The clock on the mantle chimed softly. Claudia unconsciously counted, then looked at her watch.

"Wow, it's two a.m. already!" she cried, jumping up and swigging the last of her beer. "I hate to break up the party, but I need to meet Eleanor at eight."

Deidre started to get up, but Claudia put a hand on her friend. "Don't you dare! I can see myself out." She bent down to kiss her friend on the head. "It was nice to have a chance to talk to you, Spencer."

"I should be going, as well. Can I walk you out?" he said, rising and reaching for his coat and scarf.

Patrick gathered the empty bottles and walked with them into the kitchen.

"How long are you staying, Claude?" he asked as he rinsed the bottles and placed them in the recycle bin beneath the sink.

She sighed. "I'm not sure. Dee's parents said I could stay as long as I wanted. I don't have any assignments, so there go all of my usual excuses."

"Well," Patrick said, wrapping her in a hug, "do not leave without saying goodbye."

She leaned into the hug for a moment, then pulled back. "Do you think I would do that?"

"Oh, in a heartbeat."

The night was crisp, and the moon was high. Shadows of leaves played on the sidewalk. Claudia looked around but didn't see an extra car.

"Where did you park?" she asked Spencer.

"I'm just two blocks up." He shoved his hands in his coat pockets, pushing the material down from his chest. The movement amplified the cut of his upper body and showed off the musculature hiding beneath.

Claudia's breath caught in her chest for a second before she realized she was staring. She crossed her arms in front of her chest, suddenly very aware of the cold evening.

They walked down the street in the awkward silence of two people left alone for the first time.

He paused at the driveway to Deidre's parents' garage. She stopped, thinking of a way to break the silence. But he spoke first.

"Can I ask you a personal question?"

She had taken a few steps towards the garage but turned back to him. Sucking on her teeth as she thought, Claudia shrugged. "Shoot."

"What is it about your family that keeps you away?" he asked, keeping his eyes on hers.

"Ha!" the word exploded from her mouth. "That's a conversation that needs a bottle of wine to go with it."

Spencer smiled slightly. The delicious smile made Claudia's stomach flutter. Despite the cold, she wanted to stay. She wanted to take him in as long as she could. And yet something, something she couldn't put her finger on, was pulling at her.

Maybe it was as simple as being tired out from the day or the drive the day before. Or maybe it was the itch she always had while in River Styx.

"I'm willing to pay that admission. Can I take you to dinner? Tomorrow night, well...," he stumbled over the thought, glancing at his watch. "I mean, tonight?"

"I'd like that," she agreed, rocking forward on her toes. She crinkled up her nose before adding, "But not at the Pie Hole."

"Oh no," he shook his head. "Can you imagine the looks those two would be throwing all night? I am absolutely with you there."

Claudia laughed, shoving her hands into her sweatpants pockets. "They are absurdly oblivious of their obviousness. Some things never change. Speaking of, is Mimi's still around?"

"Yes! And Mrs. Tan always has the best wine selection!"

"Then it's a deal," Claudia agreed. She began to tap the ground with the toe of one sneaker, like a horse anxious to run.

"Great!" he said, noticing her stance. "Oh gosh. I'm sorry! It's really cold out here. You go on inside."

"Thank you. I'll see you later," she turned to jog up the stairs.

"Hey!" Spencer suddenly called out. "What's your number?"

Claudia jogged back to his side, holding out her hand. He unlocked his phone and handed it to her.

"There. You've just sent me your first text." She smiled and winked before tearing up the stairs to the apartment over the garage.

He laughed, noting that she'd texted herself with a wine glass and a winking face.

Claudia and Ellie's Childhood Home

River Styx, Ohio

Thursday, March 25, this year

"WE HAVE TO WRAP this up by eleven. I have a poetry class to get to in the city," Eleanor announced, her hands on her hips. She looked more like a model for a magazine article called something like, 'How to Clean Out Mom's Attic in 10 Easy Steps,' than a real person doing so. Her bouncy, curled hair was pulled back with a pale lavender bandana that matched one of the stripes in her tucked-in flannel shirt, her jeans were hemmed to fall just below her ankles, and her gray eyes were perfectly lined with a sapphire shade of liner.

Claudia looked down at her clothes. She had blindly picked out a t-shirt that had been free from a charity outing she had photographed in Los Angeles and some jeans that she couldn't say for certain hadn't been with her since high school. Though she'd showered the evening before, her still-wet hair was twisted into a bun on top of her head.

"Yes, master," Claudia said as she followed her sister up the attic stairs.

Eleanor clicked her tongue and rolled her eyes. Climbing up the last few stairs, they surveyed the room. It was still neatly laid out, as it had been when they were children and had their playroom in the attic. One side for storage, and one side for play, with a pale lemony-colored rug.

"This is so surreal," Claudia whispered.

They had been good friends once and had spent hours playing in the attic together with the pretend kitchen and school chalkboard. But a schism had occurred, and neither could point to the precise moment it had all blown apart.

The artifacts and proof of their childhood bond were still on display in this room. Nudging past her sister, Claudia walked over and sat down in front of the small, plastic kitchen set. She opened the pretend oven and, as she had expected, found a bin of play food.

"We had so much fun up here. What happened?"

She pulled out the pieces to make a hamburger, popped it onto a plate, and held it out to her sister.

But Eleanor wasn't paying attention. She waved her hand at the offer and walked around the room, deep in thought.

"Mom said that she wanted to keep the boxes of Grandma and Grandpa's things and that there was a box of Dad's stuff that we should go through, but otherwise, we could take everything else to the second-hand shop on Maple Street."

Claudia returned the food neatly to the bin. She rubbed her hand over the sunny yellow rug. Dust in the air reflected the sunlight from the window. The curtains Alice had made - orange with small zoo animals scattered across the fabric - were still up. She breathed in, held it for a beat, then let it go.

"Do you think the kids would play with this stuff?" she asked her sister.

Eleanor looked over and cocked an eyebrow. "I highly doubt it. There aren't any screens or buttons attached. Also, they're teenage boys."

Claudia looked back at the playset, took out her phone, and snapped a quick picture. She texted it to Patrick.

Do you want this relic for the baby?

TOTALLY!

"Patrick and Deidre will take it for the baby. I'll pack it up and put it in my car," Claudia told her sister.

"Sounds good," Eleanor replied absentmindedly. "Why don't you work on the box of Dad's stuff and find our grandparents' boxes? I'll go through the rest of the toys and stuff and pack them up."

The movement was subtle, but Claudia couldn't help but feel like Eleanor had claimed territory over their past lest she give any more of it away. Silently, she packed up the play kitchen and accessories and took them out to her car.

By the time she had returned, Eleanor had already boxed and labeled a third of the remaining items.

Definitely, Claudia carried their chalkboard, plastic table, and matching chairs out to her car.

As she crested the stairs, she saw that Eleanor had pulled out a box labeled PAUL and placed it in the center of the room.

Subtle as a dump truck, as always, thought Claudia.

She sat down, cross-legged, with her back to her sister, and opened the box.

In the months after his death, Alice had divided their father's belongings with his siblings and mother. They had experienced 19 wonderful years of devotion, but she figured that the mother's desire for tokens of her child outweighed the needs of a wife. She had the best reminders that he had lived in Claudia and Eleanor.

At the top of the box was a stuffed dog, Love Pup, neatly tucked in by an old Atlanta Braves t-shirt. Claudia smiled. She knew that Alice had won the stuffed animal at the county fair when her parents were dating. He had always been tucked into the top rung of her parents' bed, and she and Eleanor had played with him on many happy nights.

She turned to show Eleanor but thought better of it.

Pulling the shirt out, Claudia held it up. It was a soft blue with a small number 31. She knew because her father had drilled it into her head that the number belonged to Greg Maddux, his favorite pitcher. It looked to be her size, so she folded it neatly and put it in the Claudia KEEP pile.

Next was a World's Best Dad mug that he had kept on his desk at the middle school where he taught English and Social Studies. Devoid of his favorite pens, Claudia decided to put it in the donate pile for the next best dad to receive.

She continued for another twenty minutes, thoughtfully keeping or discarding items from his professional and personal lives. Then she hit upon an exciting find.

"I wondered where this had gone!" she exclaimed.

"What?" Eleanor asked.

"Mom and Dad's scrapbook," Claudia said, turning around and showing off the cracked brown leather book.

Eleanor stopped labeling the box she was on and came over to look. "Oh, wow," she whispered.

The two had pooled their money together to purchase the book and supplies. It had been a present for their parents' 15th wedding anniversary.

Sitting shoulder to shoulder, the two paged through the book. It started with pictures of their parents when they were first dating. Each page had been lovingly crafted by the sisters. They stopped at a page that featured Alice and Paul's altar photo. Eleanor had cut flower petals out of paper to match the bouquet that her mom was holding in the picture. They were beautifully intricate and had managed to thwart the destructive powers of time.

Claudia ran her hand over one of the flowers. "You did such an amazing job on these. I just couldn't believe it when you showed them to me, Ellie."

Eleanor looked at her sister. A shy smile spread across her face. "Thanks."

They continued through the book, pausing to reminisce about each of the photos they had purposefully chosen. Page by page, they watched themselves grow up.

A soft digital chirp interrupted the comfortable silence.

Eleanor looked at her watch. "Oh shoot. It's 10:45 already. I have to go," she said as she surveyed the room. Her mind was already calculating the tasks yet to be done. She groaned.

"I can finish," Claudia offered.

Eleanor studied her before launching into instructions. "Remember, mom wants Grandma and Grandpa's things, but everything else can go. And…"

"I got it, Eleanor. I promise. I can do this."

"Fine," Eleanor said skeptically. She started toward the steps but paused at the top. "Thank you," she offered before continuing the walk down.

Claudia watched as her sister's head bobbed down the stairs. "You're welcome!" she called out.

The Scott House

River Styx, Ohio

Thursday, March 25, this year

ELLIE PULLED A SMALL bag of teddy bear-shaped graham crackers from her purse and opened it, a habit she hadn't gotten out of since her kids had grown into preteens. Her hair was, once again, pulled back by her bandana, and her makeup had been adjusted. She offered Nick a tiny bear cracker before popping it into her own mouth.

Today, they had skipped any pretense and just met at his house. Somehow that made it feel different. Still amazing, but different. Nick leaned over and kissed her gently on the cheek before wandering, alluringly naked, to the master bath. She busied herself with making the bed, luxuriating in the oaky smell of him on the pillows. Once that was complete, she wandered down to the kitchen to get herself a glass of water.

As she passed, she took in the photographs he had hanging on his walls and across his mantle. Many of them were of Nick and his brothers or parents. She remembered that he was the youngest of a tight-knit family. There were shots of them boating and hiking, but also what must have been wedding day photos for each brother. All of the boys looked alike: muscular, lean, dark hair turning salty over the years. The soft umber tones, variegated across the five boys, hinted at their father's Mexican heritage and their mother's African roots. Nick was assuredly the most handsome of the group, but Ellie couldn't help but admire the fine aging process that time had done on the oldest brother. She hoped that Nick would follow suit.

She paused in her thoughts. *What do I expect the future to look like?* she wondered. *Am I there, even on the periphery? Do I want to be?*

The trajectory of her marriage wasn't turning out how she had anticipated. Though she made all the right gestures and said all the right things to outsiders, her marriage to Greg had been rocky long before she had gone out seeking a medical answer to her panic attacks. She hated to say, even to herself, that things were bad. Greg wasn't abusive. He had always been a gentle, thoughtful, and sweet man.

But after she had given birth to Edward and Jacob, things with Greg had just seemed off. At first, she had let herself believe that it was something about her post-baby body that was unappealing. She'd even confronted him about it, but he insisted he still loved her deeply and blamed it on a stressful tax season. And so, being the obligatorily malleable female of the relationship, Ellie had taken him at his word and had not brought it up since.

If she had been a betting woman, she might have gambled on the idea that there was someone else. Though no amount of sleuthing had ever unearthed evidence that he was having an affair. For one thing, she could account for nearly every moment of his day. It was like clockwork: wake up, eat, pack lunch for himself and the kids, at work by 7:30 a.m., home at 4:30 p.m., dinner, homework, and video games or sports practice with the boys. No lipstick on his collar or the scent of another's cologne or perfume.

Ellie shook the thought from her mind.

Passing the formal dining room, she noted an art piece hanging over the table that could have been something Claudia had photographed.

She rolled her eyes. *Claudia.*

The old familiar jealousy rose within her. She had done everything that was asked of her, or so she felt. She had always attempted to 'choose the right' as she had been taught by her parents. Obedient, cheerful, resourceful, and pure in heart; these were the qualities she had spent her life cultivating in herself. And yet, she never failed to feel eclipsed by the rebellious spirit of Claudia.

Well, Ellie thought to herself, *who's the rebel now?*

The night of her father's funeral, Ellie had been sitting alone on the sidewalk stoop in front of her family's home when Nick emerged through the front door. She scooted to the left to give him room to walk past her, but to Ellie's surprise, he sat down next to her.

"Your sister is infuriating," he had said, breaking the silence of the cold evening.

She studied him with a side-eye before replying with a sigh. "Tell me about it."

She wrapped her bare arms into the fold of her knees and the warmth of her long, flowy, black skirt.

"Oh, Ellie! You must be freezing!" he said, taking his coat and wrapping it around her. It smelled of leather and other manly scents that left a rumbling feeling just below her stomach.

"A little," she admitted.

He followed up by putting his arm around her, jostling the coat slightly to create friction and warmth. She had been surprised when he left his hand clasping the coat around her shoulders.

"How are you doing? I don't feel like I've taken the opportunity to ask," he said.

She didn't know how to reply. Her mind and heart were a jumble of emotions. Instead, she burst into tears.

He pulled her closer, placing her head on his shoulder. His hand brushed through her hair as he murmured, "Shhh. It's okay, Ellie."

She wiped at her eyes with cold fingers before looking up at him. The streetlight caught the wetness in his eyes and made them sparkle. She reached up to wipe the tear, wondering, *Am I crossing a line?*

He had caught her hand in his and held it. He studied it for a moment, then turned his eyes back to hers.

Did she care if she crossed a line?

She leaned up, catching a small breath before pressing her unsure lips against his. Thrillingly, she felt him reciprocate, kissing her back with the same timid ferocity. Time stood still. Time flew. Their hungry kisses continued. Nick had pulled back first. He squeezed her hand.

"I'm sorry, but I have to go," he had said. She shrugged out of his coat, her heart doing cartwheels in her chest.

"Don't be sorry," she had replied. "I understand." And she watched him walk to his car and drive away.

River Styx Memorial Library

River Styx, Ohio

Thursday, March 25, this year

CLAUDIA CLOSED THE TRUNK of her car with a satisfying push. After dropping some of the toys off in the Horrigans' garage, she had made several trips to the second-hand store to donate the boxes and furniture that her mother no longer wanted. It was now a little after 4 p.m.

She stretched out her aching neck and back, wishing that the small town had a coffee shop. Stepping into her car, she noticed the pale pink house in her rearview mirror.

It had once been the home of a matchstick magnate, the founder of the town, and the primary employer for those who hadn't been farmers in the nineteenth century. The amazing structure rivaled anything found in Cleveland's famed Millionaire Row. But since the late fifties, it had been the River Styx Community Library.

Claudia was sweaty and dusty, but that wasn't an unnatural state for her. Given the amount of time she had sat waiting for the perfect picture in a desert, it was a wonder she hadn't acquired a permanent cloud of dust, like Pig-Pen from the Peanuts comic strip. She did, however, apply a lightly tinted chapstick that she kept in her car. Shrugging at her reflection in the mirror, she slammed the visor shut. She grabbed her purse and keys, locked her car, and set out on foot.

In five minutes, she was at the old front door. A bell tinkled merrily as she opened it.

"Oh, my goodness! Claudia O'Malley! Girl, come here. Let me get a look at you!" exclaimed the petite woman sitting at the front desk. Carla Fortune had been the head librarian since Claudia was a child. She had a knack for remembering each child who had passed through the door, their interests, and their favorite books. And clearly, that ability extended into their adulthood.

"Hello, Mrs. Fortune! It's so lovely to see you!" Claudia crossed to the back of the desk and bent to hug the tiny woman. She smelled like Elizabeth Taylor's perfume, Passion, the same scent Claudia remembered from her childhood.

"Oh, child. You know you're allowed to call me Carla now, don't you?" she said, holding Claudia's arms and giving her a huge smile. Claudia did the same, sizing up the woman in front of her. From her red ballet flats to her silky red blouse, she looked exactly as Claudia remembered, save for a few dozen strands of gray in her coal-black hair.

"Yes, ma'am," Claudia responded.

"No. Not ma'am. Carla."

"Yes, Carla," she replied, smiling.

"I imagine you are in town because of Carl's passing. Such a nice man. Please give your mama my condolences. Now, how can I help you, sweetie?" Carla asked, settling back on a large cushion haphazardly placed on her desk chair.

"Patrick Horrigan mentioned that Carl had purchased some of my work for the reading room, and I was down the street, so I figured I'd stop in and take a look."

"Of course! You can walk up the stairs to the third floor or take the elevator we installed a few years ago near the children's section," Carla replied.

"Thank you! It was so nice to see you," Claudia responded, turning to walk up the old staircase. The wooden structure was original to the house and had beautiful scrollwork on the railings and rungs. It smelled faintly of Murphy's Oil Soap. Studying the lovely patterns contained in the grain, Claudia was sad that she had left her camera at the garage apartment.

To Claudia's amazement and delight, the smell of coffee greeted her. To the left of the stairwell, the library had installed a small café. A young girl stood behind the counter, reading a book. She looked up when Claudia approached. "What can I make for you today?" she asked.

"I'll just have a medium coffee, please."

"Sure thing!"

Claudia looked around more as the girl poured her coffee. The third floor had been transformed into a large but cozy room. Each of the soft leather chairs had a reading lamp. Opposite the stairwell was a 360-degree fireplace, offering ambiance and warmth to all. She wandered over to the wall closest to the café. A single spotlight was trained on a print of one of her photographs. It featured a partially restored Buddhist temple from a side trip she'd taken to Wat Chiang Man when she was on assignment in Thailand.

"I guess a woman who grew up here took this photo."

Claudia jumped a mile as the girl from the counter spoke. She took the offered coffee. "Oh?" was all she said.

"Yeah, I think my mom went to school with her," the girl replied, turning back to the counter.

Claudia chuckled to herself. She wandered along the wall, pausing to study each of the prints her stepfather had chosen for the library. She was so lost in thought that it barely registered when she passed the open door of an office.

"Claudia?"

She backed up a few steps. Her face brightened. "Oh! Hello!" she said. "Is this your office?" She blushed, feeling naive and brainless as the words left her mouth.

"It is!" Spencer answered, turning slightly away from his computer. He pointed to a framed piece hanging to the left of his desk. "And look!"

Claudia stepped in. "Oh! That's a good one," she said, studying the print. "Goguryeojeong Pavilion in South Korea."

"Yes, in Achasan Park. Fun fact: it is the only place, among your pieces, I have been."

Marnie Falconer

"You've been to Korea?" she asked.

"I have," Spencer replied, smiling. "It's a long story, or, as you would say, a 'wine conversation'."

"Well, I'd love to hear it over dinner," Claudia replied.

"Speaking of dinner, I didn't expect to see you so soon."

Claudia rocked back on her heels, feeling a little embarrassed. "I was dropping off some stuff at the second-hand store and decided to run in and see..."

"Your work?" Spencer offered slyly.

She held her coffee cup up and pointed. "Yes. But more importantly, no one told me that there was good coffee to be had here. So it wasn't a total vanity trip."

He laughed.

"And now that I've seen what is, apparently, my entire legacy here in town, I should be going."

"I'm glad you stopped by, Claudia," Spencer said.

"Me too," she replied, her heart skipping in her chest. If her feet touched the ground as she walked down the stairs, it would have been news to her. She felt as young as the girl behind the coffee counter.

71

Mimi's Italian Restaurant

River Styx, Ohio

Thursday, March 25, this year

CLAUDIA HADN'T BEEN ON a real, true date in a long time. She'd gone out with men, of course, but life was more casual and free-flowing when you usually found yourself a stranger in a strange land.

And so, when she had returned to the garage apartment, she realized that the only nice clothes she had with her were the black blouse and pencil skirt she'd worn to the calling hours and a long black dress. Fortunately, she was the same height and frame as Deidre's mom, Caty.

Caty also had amazing taste.

Now, she was standing before a full-length mirror, studying herself. She had borrowed a silky red sheath dress with embroidered black roses climbing up the skirt and over the shoulder. She'd paired it with her black leather jacket, some black thigh highs, and black heels. Thankful that she'd washed her hair the night before, she had pulled it back into a series of collected curly puffs, creating a kind of mohawk braid down her head and upper back.

She checked one last time to make sure that she didn't have lipstick on her teeth and left.

They had decided to meet at the restaurant since Spencer would be coming from work just a block away. He was waiting at the door for her and had changed into an icy blue shirt and added a gray sportscoat. His smile made the annoying hosiery bearable.

She returned the smile.

"After you," he said, holding open the door.

Mimi's had not changed at all. It had been 'the' first date spot in high school. The smell of homemade garlic bread met them at the door. Claudia breathed in and sighed. Spencer just nodded in agreement.

A hostess showed them the way to a table in the back. They ordered a bottle of cabernet and settled in. Claudia looked around. Each table was covered in a red checked tablecloth, with a single hurricane lamp offering an intimate glow.

She turned her attention to Spencer. "Korea?" she questioned.

"Uh-uh. You first," he replied as the waiter poured the first round and sat the wine glasses in front of them.

"Ugh. Where to start?" she said, lifting her glass to take a sip. She reached back and pulled her hair forward to play with the ends thoughtfully. "How well do you know Eleanor?"

"Well," started Spencer, "I knew Carl more than anyone since he volunteered at the library. And through him, I'd hear stories of your sister, Alice, and sometimes, you." He paused to take a sip. Claudia studied him as he rubbed his lips to clear the remainder of the wine. He bit his lip slightly as he thought. "Most of my interactions with her has been when she brings the kids in, though I have gone golfing with Greg a couple of times. He seems genuinely nice. From what I gather, they met after college?"

Claudia nodded.

"Eleanor strikes me as a person who is annoyed to be picking up the slack but wouldn't have it any other way," he continued. "She's kind, but I could see where she might be a bit...bristly."

"Yes, that's very astute. I hadn't thought of it that way before, but yes. She will grudgingly take on the task no one else will, but you better not forget that she did it when no one else would. I'm trying to be diplomatic, but she tends to make me crazy."

Spencer laughed. "Isn't that just the nature of siblings?" he asked.

"I guess," Claudia replied. She emptied her glass and reached for the bottle to pour herself another. "My mother and Eleanor are obsessed with the appearance of things being a certain way, from the way they interact with people to the way they dress. And very often, they impose that vision on the people around them, with or without their consent. That is just not my style. I suppose I can't fault Eleanor. It's the way we were raised."

The waiter returned with a basket of bread, and they ordered their meals.

"I feel overwhelmed by their judgment and find it easier to continue to love them from another state. When I first left, it was so easy to unknot any ties that bound me to home. My mom needed her own space at the time. Eleanor and I were already salty toward each other. The only two people in River Styx who held any sort of grip on me were Deidre and Patrick. But even they were occupied by each other and the restaurant. So, it was just more exciting to spend the holidays photographing ancient ruins rather than coming home."

She paused, placing her hands on the table to anchor herself. "Plus, I was a total daddy's girl, and after he died, I questioned a lot of things." Claudia hadn't opened up in a long time. It was surprising to see how easily everything she kept inside spilled out. Spencer reached over and squeezed her hand. She squeezed back.

"How old were you when your dad died?" he asked.

"Seventeen," she replied. "He was only 39. It seemed so old back then. Now…," she drifted off.

"Now you know. It's like no time has passed," he offered.

"Right!" she said, wiping gingerly at a tear that had started to form in her eye. She quietly studied her napkin. After that morning's interaction, Claudia wasn't sure how to feel about her relationship with her sister. As annoyed as she could get by some of Eleanor's behaviors, she truly wanted to find a way to be companionable, if not close. She knew that her schedule contributed to an easy out from making the effort. Maybe now was the time to change that.

"So, Korea?"

He took a deep breath. "Korea," he agreed, taking a long sip of his wine.

"I dated the same girl all through college, Meredith - Meri. We met on our first day of freshman year. We both worked at the library. Things progressed, as they do, and by senior year, we were living together in a little apartment off-campus." Spencer paused to exhale. Claudia leaned in, her root-beer-colored eyes intent on his. Several emotions flashed across his face before he went on.

"Right before Christmas break, Meri told me she was pregnant. I was really excited. I'd already bought a ring and was planning to propose, so I figured it was just fine. That the universe was saying that we were meant to be. But in February, she lost the baby," he shook his head and took another drink.

"I want to say that I tried hard to be supportive in the months afterward, but I just don't know. Everything was kinda foggy. I put a lot of energy into finishing my classes. I spent a lot of time writing my final papers at a local coffee shop. If I wasn't in class, I was usually there. That last week of college, I had ordered a book through another college, and I had to pick it up in a different part of the library. So, as I was walking to the inter-library loan desk, I had to pass a series of little breakout rooms, and in one, I saw Meri with a doctoral candidate from her program," he stopped to clear his throat. "Studying anatomy, if you will."

"Oh, Spencer!" Claudia whispered.

"I didn't know what to do, so I just turned right around and went back to the apartment. When she got home, I confronted her. She didn't deny it. Of course, she said they were in love, and she hadn't wanted to hurt me more. Then she left to think about things.

"I called one of my buddies from home. He was packing to go to South Korea the next morning. It was a graduation present from his grandparents, who had emigrated from there. I checked with the airline, and there was one more seat, so I bought it. I sent my final papers in as they were. I didn't have any exams, so I was technically done with school. I packed up anything that was really and truly mine, shipped it to my parents' house, and left her the rest.

"We caught up at LAX, my friend and I. We spent three weeks exploring Korea. It was amazing. And extremely healing." He sat back, breaking the spell.

Claudia spoke first. "Well, this bottle is certainly on me tonight. That was definitely much more of a wine conversation."

Spencer simpered, giving her the courage to go on.

"I guess I don't understand, though. Why would you want that reminder in your office with you?"

He finished the last of his wine and reached for the bottle. "It was, most assuredly, the lowest point in my life. But it didn't break me. And your photo serves as a reminder of that. Every decision in my past has led me here. And I wouldn't be who I am today without those experiences. Good or bad."

Claudia's cell phone buzzed. Offering an apologetic glance, she looked at the caller. "It's Patrick," she said. Spencer motioned for her to pick up. She did.

"Claude? I'm with Dee at the hospital. She's...," Patrick sobbed into the phone. Claudia motioned for the waiter, signaling that she needed her bill. "I think there's something wrong."

"I'll be right there, Patrick," she said, clicking off. She looked at Spencer. Her concern was mirrored in his face.

"Deidre?" he asked.

"Yes, I'm so sorry. I have to go," she said, gathering her coat and purse.

"I've got the bill," he replied. "You go. I'll catch up with you later."

Caduceus Hospital - Maternity Triage
Poe City Limits, Ohio
Thursday, March 25, this year

CLAUDIA FOUND PATRICK IN the waiting room of the maternity section. He was scrunched in the chair, his elbows on his knees, his fingers laced in his hair. He looked up at the sound of her heel clicks. His eyes were bloodshot, his face puffy. She ran to him, falling to her knees in front of his chair.

"Patrick?" she asked expectantly.

He reached out and pulled her into a shaky embrace. "They're okay," he sobbed. "They're okay. But I was so scared, Claude."

She held on to him as he wept, rubbing his back lightly as though he, himself, were a baby. "What happened?" she asked.

He sat up and pulled a crumpled tissue from his sweatshirt pocket. "Around three or so, Dee didn't feel good, so she went home to lie down. That's not so unusual. She's been getting tired more and more lately. But then she started vomiting, and she couldn't stop." He paused to blow his nose and clear his throat. "Caty brought her here, and I met them as soon as I could."

"But what was wrong?" Claudia asked, feeling completely out of her comfort zone.

"The doctors say that she'd gotten too dehydrated. Which can be dangerous in the last trimester, but everything checks out now. She's resting and getting an IV of fluid right now." He ran his fingers back through his hair. The tissue lay forgotten on his lap.

Claudia sat in the chair next to him and reached for his hand. He studied her fingers, laced with his own.

"Had Dee told you about the other pregnancies?" he asked quietly.

Claudia was thrown but managed to stammer, "No."

"She's...we've lost three - always in the first 15 or so weeks," he paused and sighed. "I think she didn't want to burden you. We talk about it, of course, but I don't think she's confided in anyone else besides her mom. After the second time, they ran us both through so many tests. And it came back that she has this clotting disorder, uh, APC resistance. It's supposed to be common in Asian families.

But, Christ, I was so scared, seeing her in that hospital bed again. I didn't know what to do."

Patrick started to cry again.

"Wait? What does a clotting disorder mean?" Claudia started. She waited for an answer while he blew his nose.

"We have this regimen of shots and meds that she has to do every day. It worked this time. We still have our peanut. But it's been really hard on her."

"I'm sorry," Claudia said as tears slid from her eyes. "I haven't been there for you or her. I haven't been such a great friend. I know there's only so much that can be conveyed in intermittent FaceTime calls."

"Claude, that's not what I'm - " he started, but she interrupted him.

"I know. But I had to say it. I've been thinking about it a lot over the past few days."

"Patrick, Claudia?"

They both looked up. Caty was standing in the doorway, motioning for them. They walked through the security door to the maternity area and down the hall to a small triage room.

Deidre looked so small in the huge hospital bed. She had a bluish cast in the industrial lighting, but her eyes were bright and smiling. Claudia stepped in, awkwardly staring at first. Then, she reached over the IV tubes to hug her friend tightly. She ran her hand lovingly on Deidre's alabaster cheek.

"I don't know what to say," she confided.

"How about starting with the fact that you were on a *date* with Spencer?" Deidre teased. Her eyes crinkled as she laughed. Claudia looked at Caty, who shrugged and put her arm around her son-in-law.

Claudia rolled her eyes. "Yes, that sounds like the perfect place to start," she replied, giving Deidre's cheek a playful slap. "What am I going to do with you?"

"Just love me," Deidre replied. She yawned and closed her eyes.

"The doctor is giving her fluids, but she's free to go when that is done. She'll need to take it easy for the next couple of weeks," Caty offered.

A soft snore came from the bed. Claudia hugged Patrick again and left him with his sleeping wife. She motioned for Caty to join her.

"I've been thinking, I don't have anything lined up for the next few weeks. I was going to go back to Pittsburgh, but I think I'd like to stay here if you don't mind me taking over your garage for a bit?" A plan had been circling in the back of her mind, but the details hadn't become clear until she saw Deidre.

"Of course, sweetie. You know we're happy to have you," Caty responded.

"I'm happy to pay you," Claudia offered.

"Don't even think about it, although, can you do two things for me?"

"Name them!"

"I know my daughter, and I need you to help her relax. I'm sure she'll want to be at the restaurant, but maybe between you and Patrick, you can convince her to take it easy."

"Done!" Claudia agreed. "And the second thing?"

"You have to tell Alice," Caty replied, pulling Claudia into a hug.

Claudia made a face at her. Caty laughed.

"Yes, ma'am."

The Kouris Home

River Styx, Ohio

Thursday, March 25, this year

ELLIE WAS LOST IN thought, her hands inside pink dishwashing gloves and submerged in the soapy water in her kitchen sink. She only had a few drinking glasses and two pans left to wash and dry. As a child, her mother's dishwasher had clouded all of the clear glasses, so Ellie could never bear to wash her beautiful vintage-styled glassware in the machine. Plastic-anytime-cups could go in, but never the dinner glasses. And woe to any of the men in her house who did it wrong!

Greg and the boys were playing some video game in the living room, the music just loud enough to be heard above the running dishwasher. She quietly hummed along as she moved from one task to another.

Her phone chimed with an incoming message, startling her and causing her to drop the glass she was drying. It hit the edge of the countertop with a bang before shattering on the tile floor.

"Babe?" Greg called from the couch. "Is everything okay?"

She took a deep breath and held it. Then, let it out slowly. "Yes, hun. Just dropped one of the glasses."

With one athletic move, Greg lept over the back of the couch and was quickly behind her with the broom and dustpan. "I'll get this," he said. "You go relax."

"Dad! We can't finish this guy without you," thirteen-year-old Jacob called from the living room floor.

"This will just take a minute," Greg replied as Ellie slid her phone into her back pocket. "Hey, while we are paused, why don't you two gather up the rest of the house trash and roll the can out to the curb?"

There was a small amount of grumbling from Jacob, but her older son, Eddie, simply cuffed him lightly on the back of the head, and it stopped.

"I'll get the basement; you get the upstairs?" Eddie said to his brother as they pulled new trash bags from the storage shelf in the closet.

Ellie watched her boys, her heart full. She adored them and was proud of how they were maturing into young men, still mixed with a bit of little boy snuggles. They were so much like Greg in looks and demeanor, just as she had hoped when they were babies.

Conflicted, she turned to look at her husband, who was bagging up the last of the broken glassware. His dark hair had become a little more salty with age, but his physique remained that of an athlete. True, he'd traded football for golf as he'd gotten older, but that had been just fine by her.

He caught her staring and smiled. "What?" he inquired, leaning on the kitchen peninsula.

"Nothing," Ellie replied, cupping his face in her hand and kissing his forehead. "I could have gotten it, but thank you for cleaning that up." She picked up the romance book that she had left on the end of the counter. "If you don't mind, I think I will go upstairs and read a bit."

"Of course not. I've got things down here. You go enjoy your book. Beachy setting? I know you love imagining a beach on a blah March day."

Ellie smiled, absentmindedly. "What? Oh. The book. Yes, it takes place in coastal Georgia."

"Nice," Greg responded as he pulled the stopper on the kitchen sink to let the dishwater drain.

She passed Jacob on the stairs and ruffled his hair. He smiled at her, and his smile reminded her of her father's. Her heart swelled as she smiled back. She continued up the stairs to her room as her boys regrouped in front of the TV.

She pulled her phone out as she sat on her soft, lacy, white bed linens and tapped the messaging app.

> 💬 Hey you :) Was finishing up checking on some patients at the hospital and saw Claudia and her friend, Peter (?) in the Maternity Triage waiting room. Just thought you should know.

Ellie thought for a second. *Who was Peter?*

> 💬 Patrick Horrigan?

She texted back. The thought bubbles popped up in the messaging app as Nick wrote his response.

💬 Sorry, yes. His name was not coming to me.

Ellie responded.

💬 Mystery solved. Ok. Deidre is expecting, she must be pretty close. I hope everything is okay.

💬 You could ask your sister. I've got to go, driving home. 😘 Chat with you more tomorrow?

Ellie smiled at the emoji. She knew that when he was coming down from doctor mode, Nick shut everything else out. So, while she would have loved to take some time to text with him tonight, it wasn't going to happen. She sighed and deleted the chat stream, as she almost always did with his messages.

She lay her head down on her pillow and thought about playing pretend as a child with Deidre and her sister. She did hope everything was okay but had no desire to ask her sister about it. Plus, how would she explain where she had gotten the information?

The Siegel House

River Styx, Ohio

Thursday, March 25, this year

CLAUDIA CHECKED HER PHONE when she got to the car. There were two messages from Spencer.

💬 How are D and the baby?

💬 I brought a bottle of the cabernet home. Want to come by and talk?

She studied her rumpled dress and smeared eyeliner. The dress needed a good steam, but the makeup could be touched up.

💬 D and baby are good. Dehydration! She needs to take it easy (ha!) Also, you had me at "cab." Send me your address.

With his address pulled up on her GPS, Claudia started her car. As she drove the familiar streets, she thought about what Patrick had confided in her. Deidre and Patrick had been together so long Claudia often wondered why they hadn't started a family. She had just chalked it up to running a business. Why hadn't Deidre told her about the other pregnancies?

She remembered that Eleanor hadn't told anyone about being pregnant until she'd passed 13 weeks. Maybe it had something to do with that? Either way, Claudia had come to realize that she wanted to re-engage with her family and friends. She wanted to really and truly be a part of their lives. And that meant facing all of her ghosts in River Styx.

Spencer's house was one of the newer ones on his street, with a nice lawn and minimal garden beds. The front view of the house was predominantly taken up by the double garage door, but a welcoming sidewalk led the way to a small porch and front door, just off to the side.

She knocked on the screen door just as he opened the heavy inner door. They smiled at one another as he gestured for her to come in.

"Let me take your coat?" he offered. He hung it up in the coat closet as she sat her purse down on the bottom step of the carpeted stairway leading to a second level and turned to survey the room.

The walls were pale, mossy green, and the layout opened through a dining space and into the kitchen. His furniture was sparse but tasteful. It had probably been set up at the department store in that exact fashion, but, strangely, that made Claudia adore it more.

Spencer had the bottle of cabernet breathing on the kitchen counter. He grabbed it and pulled two glasses from the cabinet. "What's going on with Deidre?"

Claudia took the glass he offered and sat gingerly on the corner of the couch. "She was extremely dehydrated, which, I gather, can jump-start the birth process. She is getting an IV of fluids and will have to take it easy in the next few weeks. So, scary and potentially bad, but taken care of for now."

"And the baby?" he asked, folding one leg up to sit facing her from the other side of the couch.

"The baby is fine." As soon as the words left her mouth, Claudia burst into tears.

"Oh my! Claudia, are you okay?" He put his glass down on the coffee table and scooted closer, offering her a tissue from a box he pulled off the sofa table.

"I'm so sorry. I'm not usually a mess like this! I think it just hit me what might have happened."

Spencer pulled her close as she sobbed. His hands brushed through the strands that had escaped from her clipped-back hair. "Shhh. Shhh. It's okay," he murmured.

She reached her hand up to his lips to quiet his murmuring. He kissed her fingers. It felt electric. She moved her hand into his hair and pulled his lips to hers. Her heart pounded as they made contact. Their tongues brushed, and she felt a nip of his teeth on her bottom lip. He laid a trail of kisses down her jaw and neck, pausing at the top of her cleavage.

Claudia rocked across her left knee and threw her right leg over Spencer's lap. Her dress hiked up, exposing the garters holding her hosiery on.

He groaned appreciatively. "Claudia?" he asked between breaths and kisses. "Are you sure?"

She kissed him hard, her fingers laced through his soft hair. *Did he just request consent?* she thought to herself.

"Yes. Yes, Spencer. I'm sure."

Slowly, he ran his thumbs over the silky black fabric, then under the ribbons to snap open her thigh-highs. His mouth retraced the path he'd taken down her clavicle. She slid forward until the satin of her panties connected with the prominence of his slacks. Claudia rode the wave of her thrill between the feel of the satin and his hardening length. As she did, he reached back and unzipped her dress, pulling her breasts out. He leaned in and sucked on an exposed nipple, sending her nearly crashing into climax.

Sensing this final height, Spencer stood up, lifting Claudia with him. She wrapped her legs around his lean middle as he carried her up to his room on the second floor. He returned to her mouth, kissing her with each step.

Laying her gently on the bed, he removed her black panties, kissing her legs as he pulled them down. He took off his pants and boxers. With a quivering hand, he stroked his uncircumcised dick a few times, before he plunged into her. They moved together to completion.

Sighing, she snuggled into the crook of his arm. Her fingers lightly traced the muscular curve of his chest. They settled into silence. She wasn't even sure he was awake until he spoke.

"You are amazing," he murmured into her hair.

Claudia smiled. "You were everything I thought you would be, with your sexy mouth and bewitching eyes."

"My teeth are crooked," he laughed.

She raised on one elbow and kissed his full lips and ever so slightly crooked front tooth. "But, damn! Is that hot," she smiled, settling back into his embrace. He pulled the sheet over the top of them. The warmth and smell of him made her stomach flutter. She softly rubbed her thigh against his, thinking. They remained like that for some time.

Spencer smiled. "A penny for your thoughts?" he said.

She sighed. "I want to talk to you about something, but I'm not sure how to approach it."

"This isn't where you confess that you have an unknowable number of husbands stashed across the globe, is it?"

"Of course not," she said, tickling his side. He removed his arm from behind her head, trying to get away from her moving fingers. Adjusting the sheet, he rolled over to face her. His eyes studied her seriously.

"Then what is it?"

"I've been thinking about coming home for a little while."

"Home? Like River Styx? Here?"

"Yes."

"And, you are worried about telling me...because?"

"If you had planned on making this a one-time thing, it's going to be awkward when I run into you at the supermarket."

"I would like for this to be more than a one-time thing, Claudia."

She blushed at the sound of her name. "Good. Me, too." She leaned in and kissed his lips. He pulled her closer to him and ignited the fire once again.

Claudia and Ellie's Childhood Home

River Styx, Ohio

Sunday, March 28, this year

"HI, MOM."

It had felt strange to knock on the door of her childhood home, but Claudia wasn't sure of the protocol anymore. She'd spent the past three days hiding in the apartment, mostly working on cleaning and uploading images to various stock photo services and the other projects she did when she wasn't in the field.

"Claudia? Come in, come in."

Giving her a quizzical look, Alice moved into the house. She was dressed in sweatpants that Claudia recognized from childhood and a sweatshirt that said, "Grandmas are antique little girls." The television was on, quietly playing some afternoon game show. Alice sat down in a recliner and motioned to the couch.

"I didn't get around to thanking you for cleaning out the attic," she said, picking up her mug of tea. Alice suddenly looked old and tired. Why hadn't Claudia noticed before?

"You're welcome," Claudia offered, slightly taken aback. "I came by because I wanted to let you know that I'm going to stay in town for a little while," she told her mother.

"Oh?"

"Yes, well, Deidre had a bit of a scare a few nights ago, and I had already been thinking that I might stay to help her in any way that I can."

"Well, you are more than welcome to the guest bedroom."

"Oh! Thank you, but Caty offered their apartment. I don't want to impose on you. Plus, the apartment allows me to come and go as I need to without bothering anyone."

"Claudia, you are never an imposition or a bother to me."

"Oh, I didn't - "

"May I be candid with you?"

Claudia nodded.

"You need to lose this childish idea that it's you against me. We all make choices. When you were younger, as your mother, I felt the direct impact of yours. And, on more than one occasion, I had a little more insight than you did at the time. But, still, those were your choices to make. I've had my own, for good or for bad. I love you desperately and am proud of you. Maybe I should have said it more." A tear rolled down her cheek. She wiped it away with her ring finger. Claudia noticed that she was wearing two sets of wedding bands on her left hand. She recognized the simpler set as the one from her father.

"You have always been my smart, brave girl. If I gave you the impression that you were anything but that, I'm sorry. I know that I can be overwhelmingly brash sometimes. Your father used to tease me about it."

Claudia walked over to the recliner and leaned in to hug her mother. She was struck again by how tiny the woman seemed to be. Sitting on the edge of the chair's arm, she took Alice's hand. "Honestly, Mom, that's part of the reason I want to stick around for a bit. I've worked hard, and I've done a lot of adventurous, amazing things. But I've neglected this part of me for a long time."

"Honey, I can't tell you how happy I am to hear that. And if you want to stay with Caty and Stanton, I completely understand." Alice put her tea down on the end table and leaned towards her daughter. Her eyes sparkled. "I'm going to tell you a secret. I haven't even told your sister yet," she confided. "I put money down on a condo out past the high school. It's a new senior living community. No yard work. It has a pool, a rec center, and a big community room. It's perfect. I'm getting too old to live alone in this house."

"Wow. Mom. I am speechless."

"I'm sure your sister won't be. She'll try to talk me out of it."

"Is that why you had us clean the attic?"

"Yes. Well, that and I started to do it four or five times but didn't want to traipse up and down those narrow stairs."

"When will you move to the new condo?"

"In about two weeks."

"So soon?"

"Honey, I've buried two husbands already. Life isn't going to slow down any time soon."

"Oh! Well, is there anything else I can do to help you?"

"I've already made arrangements with a moving company. But thank you."

They sat for a few hours in companionable silence, watching game shows and occasionally shouting out the answers to the trivia questions. Claudia felt a piece of her overwhelming weight slowly evaporating. Her mother was right. They were both adult women now, and while it was clear that she would always voice her opinions on what Claudia did, Alice wasn't going to stand in her way.

The Valley Café
Poe City Limits, Ohio

Monday, March 29, this year

"I'M NOT QUITE SURE how to phrase this…"

Noting the level of concern in her voice, Nick put his phone screen down on the table and looked up at Ellie. He smiled and took her hand, pausing briefly enough to look at her soft yellow manicure.

"Ellie, what is it?"

Ellie feigned interest in the mandarin orange she had speared from her salad just before speaking. Sighing, she looked back up and into his tantalizing eyes. "I want to know about your other relationships. Surely, there have been women in your life, but…I mean, you know all about me, of course. I'm just curious about you and your world."

Nick leaned back in his chair, letting go of her hand. For a moment, he looked out the window of the downtown café where they had met for lunch. Ellie studied his jaw, the way he ran his index finger along the thin line between cheek and neck. She was worried that she had asked the absolute wrong question. She desperately wanted to reach out for his hand again, to run her fingers down his cheeks. Instead, she gripped them together under the table. She was startled when Nick began to speak.

"You grew up where I did, so I'm sure you know the importance that our parents put on the idea of family. But all I ever wanted to do was practice medicine." He leaned forward and began to twist his glass in the sweat circle it had created on the table. "I watched my brothers bring home their first or second girlfriend from college, only to immediately get married and start families of their own. But, after your sister and I broke up, I was just very focused on finishing my undergrad and getting into the best possible medical school.

"Then, as I moved into my residency for cardiothoracic surgery, I began to comprehend just how little time I would have to devote to curating a relationship. Heck, even here, with you, I'm sure you've seen how distracted I can get by the cases and patients I'm covering. And I wasn't willing to introduce that into a long-term partnership, like a marriage. It's not fair. This is not to say that there haven't been dalliances or little relationships born out of convenience. But nothing that would have stood up to the scrutiny of my mother, honestly."

At this, Ellie, who had been twisting her fingers into knots, looked him dead in the eye. "Am I a dalliance?"

Nick left his seat and moved around the table to sit next to her. He took her hand. She could smell his cologne coupled with a soft note of antiseptic wash.

"No. Oh, lord, Ellie. No."

She melted into him, and he pulled her close. "Okay. Okay. It's just...I...I've put a lot on the line to be here with you. With you, period. And I don't know what this is, or what it becomes, or doesn't become. But I couldn't bear the thought of just being the flavor of the season. I won't."

"You're not, Ellie. I don't know where this goes, either. But I want to have you in my life. If that's what you want, too." He ran his fingers through her hair softly. "And I understand the predicament I've put you in with Greg and your sons. But I think, based on what you've shared, that your marriage was done a while ago. You, yourself, said that it's been nearly 2 years since you and he had a real marital relationship."

Ellie inhaled sharply and poked her head up, meeting his eyes.

"Now, don't get all huffy. You know I didn't mean anything by that. I'm just pointing out that you have been standing on the precipice of change, and you are the only one who can decide on which way to go."

"I know. But I can't leave. I can't do that to my boys."

"I'm not asking that of you."

"And, I'm afraid. I don't know how I would stand on my own two feet. I haven't worked in...," she did the math in her head, "Fifteen years!"

"If that's the way you want to go, we can figure it all out."

Her heart was beating out of control. She felt trapped and nauseous. Surely Nick could see the symptoms? She pushed his arms off of her and frantically grabbed her purse.

"I'm sorry," she whispered. "I have to go."

When she was safely in her car, she put her head on the wheel and sobbed. It took a great deal of willpower, but she finally forced her breathing into a more rhythmic pattern.

"Well," she said aloud, startling herself. "That did not go as planned."

She craved comfort, but there was no one she could talk to about this. What was she going to do? Call up Alice? 'Hey, mom, remember that guy, Nick Scott? Well, we're having an affair! Isn't that neat? I'm pretty sure that I'm in love with him. Yeah, the kind of love that makes you dizzy and giddy, but still, your heart feels full and content and seen. So, what do you think I should do about the guy I'm married to? Thoughts?'

No.

She would just have to reason her way through this, as she had, seemingly, for her entire life. Suddenly, she envied the relationship that Claudia still enjoyed with Deidre and Patrick. Despite all her time away, they were still as thick as thieves. Tired of aiming her anger and disappointment rightfully at herself, the thought allowed her an opportunity to place it all back on her sister.

She inhaled deeply and put her car into reverse. As she drove out of the parking lot, she noted that Nick's BMW was still there. She was torn between not caring and caring too deeply.

The Pie Hole

River Styx, Ohio

Monday, March 29, this year

MONDAY NIGHTS WERE KARAOKE at the Pie Hole.

Deidre and Spencer were sitting at a table near the restrooms when Claudia walked in. Patrick had just brought his wife a refill of water. He hugged Claudia as he made his way back to the bar.

The place was packed. She sat down in between her two companions, pulled her camera out of her bag, and set it on her lap.

"I had no idea it could get this crowded in here!" she said, leaning into Deidre to be heard. Deidre had one hand absent-mindedly on her stomach and her feet up on the fourth chair at the table. She sat her glass of water down on a colorful coaster.

"Oh yes. It's the best people-watching night!" She laughed.

Spencer leaned in and kissed Claudia on the cheek. She smiled, her heart exploding in her chest. "Hi," he said, giving her hand a quick squeeze.

"Hi," she returned.

Deidre watched them, grinning.

"Oh, shut up," Claudia said to her best friend.

Deidre simply stuck her tongue out.

Patrick reappeared with a whiskey, neat, and sat it in front of Claudia.

"Mom wants to know if you told Alice yet," Deidre inquired.

"I have," Claudia answered. "I went over yesterday."

"And?"

"And it went surprisingly well. We might even be on a different footing with each other. Oh! And I found out that she put money down on a condo!"

"What!" Deidre shrieked. Claudia shushed her as several of the patrons around them turned to look at them.

"Yeah, it's out by the high school somewhere. She said she's getting too old to keep the house up by herself. Which, I think, is perfectly reasonable. And! And she hasn't told Eleanor yet."

"What!" Deidre shrieked again. Claudia clamped her hand over Deidre's mouth. She smiled at the people who had turned around to give them a second dirty look. "I'm not removing my hand until you promise to let these nice customers enjoy their drinks and soppy love songs."

Deidre nodded her head in the affirmative. "She told you first?" she asked.

"Yes. Apparently, I'm not the only person Eleanor thinks she rules over. And my mother hasn't wanted to deal with her."

Deidre nodded. "Sure, that checks out."

Spencer reached over, interrupting the two. "Claudia, I think the emcee is calling for you."

Claudia looked up, confused. Patrick was standing behind her, pointing down. "Here she is, Billy," he said, grinning. Deidre covered her mouth as she snorted happily.

"What have you two...?" she asked, standing up.

"Let's welcome Claudia to the stage, she's a first-timer here, I'm told," said Billy, the emcee.

Standing, Claudia gave them each a quizzical look. Spencer shook his head, apparently not in on the joke. Patrick slipped into her seat, reaching over to rub his wife's back.

Claudia walked up to the microphone. The screen in front of her booted up: KEEP ON LOVING YOU, in the style of REO Speedwagon. She sighed and leaned into the mic.

"Let's all give your bartender a nice round of applause. He thinks he's funny; he's wrong, but he does pour a great drink." The crowd broke out into catcalls and applause. Patrick stood up and waved, still smiling at Claudia.

"Okay. Clue me in," Spencer inquired of Deidre and Patrick as the music began.

"Sophomore year talent show. We were obsessed with The Donnas' version of this song. Obsessed," Deidre began. "And Claudia convinced us to play this song for the talent show. She was Donna A, the singer. I played cymbals in the marching band, so, of course, I was Donna C. And Patrick played bass, so he was Donna F. And, yes, it did include a bit of drag on his part." She put her finger to her lips, then pointed to the stage as Claudia was coming up to the second verse.

Spencer watched silently for a bit. Then he turned to Patrick and Deidre with an unbelieving look. "She's pretty good!"

They both just smiled knowingly. Patrick picked up Claudia's camera. He was already on her bad side for this stunt and using her camera wasn't going to change his position. He snapped off a few quick photos as she indulged her friends by hamming it up.

As her last note faded, she bowed and blew kisses into the crowd. She returned to their table, pointing to Deidre and Patrick, mouthing, 'You're dead to me.' Arriving near Spencer, she leaned over and whispered, "The jury is still out on you." But she was smiling as she took Patrick's place at the table.

"You were amazing!" Spencer offered.

"Thank you, but don't get used to that." She picked up her camera and paged through the shots. She turned one toward Deidre. "He didn't do half bad. The composition is a bit different than what I would have done, but it's not bad. Just different.

"Oh! And Sarah Marie is sitting over in that corner," Claudia tossed out, pointing toward the main entrance. "If we're reminiscing about tenth-grade shenanigans, I will not hesitate to plant some seeds in her head about the direction of your marriage should you two do that again."

Deidre feigned shock. Claudia laughed. After a few seconds of bluster, Deidre joined her. Spencer just shook his head, smiling.

Claudia picked up her friend's hand. "I love you," she confided, squeezing her hand.

"I love you, too," Deidre returned, squeezing her hand back.

The Pie Hole

River Styx, Ohio

Friday, April 2, this year

"ARE YOU SURE ABOUT this?" Patrick asked Claudia.

She pulled her hair back into a ponytail and straightened her new waitress apron.

"Yes, sir! Sir!" she replied.

"Okay," he replied. "And Claudia?"

"Patrick?"

"No flipping the bottles. You are not in that movie, *Cocktail*."

Claudia gave an exasperated sigh and a covert middle finger to Patrick as he walked to the door.

"Remember. You are not Tom Cruise," he shouted as he walked out of the door. Claudia chuckled as she turned to survey the empty room. Taking a deep breath, she walked to the front door of the Pie Hole and unlocked it.

When Deidre had asked Claudia if she could sub in at the restaurant while they went to an ultrasound appointment, Claudia was happy to help her friends. After all, that was partially the reason she was staying in town. Plus she wasn't alone. Three seasoned staff members, Annie, Doug, and Mateo, were ready to go. She was just handling the bar and take-out orders.

You have trekked across the desert in a caravan of armed guards. How hard can this be?

The bell above the door tinkled as she was walking back to the bar area. She looked over her shoulder with a great customer service smile.

"Good afternoon!" she called.

"Well, howdy, pretty lady. What's a man gotta do to get some service in this here joint?"

She spun on her heel to face the customer full-on. It was Spencer. She laughed as she slid behind the bar.

"Of all the gin joints in all the towns in all the world, you had to walk into mine. Well, my friends'." She leaned up and over the bar, and he came in for a kiss.

"Did you come for lunch?" she asked.

"How could I resist an opportunity to have lunch with you?" he responded.

Patrick had taken mercy on her and was offering a simple, special menu for the day. Despite her limited restaurant experience - she had never worked at one before

- Claudia felt she could handle ringing up panini-styled grilled cheese sandwiches, bagging ready-made salads, and ladling out soup.

Thirty minutes in, she was overrun by two large take-out orders.

After fifty minutes, Spencer was taking phone orders, and a line was beginning to form.

At 12:30, like magic, everyone was gone.

Claudia breathed deeply, with a new appreciation for her friends' career. She adjusted her ponytail, which had slipped its band, and leaned back against the bar to look at Spencer. His seafoam green work shirt was unbuttoned and had come untucked from his Dockers. There was a slight soup stain under his right pectoral and a piece of lettuce dangling from his hair. He looked delicious in so many ways. Her breath caught in her chest. She tried to figure out if they had time, like two teenagers, for a quickie in the stock room. Instead, she laughed and picked the lettuce out of Spencer's hair.

She had just poured them each a shot when Patrick and Deidre walked in.

"Claudia Paige! Are you drinking your pay?" Patrick teased.

"I earned this. Besides, you aren't paying me," she stated as she tossed back the amber liquid. Spencer just offered a silent salute with his shot glass.

"And she pulled you into this, too, Spencer?" he said, feigning shock.

"Would you look at the time?" Spencer replied, tucking his shirt back into his pants. He kissed Claudia on the cheek and offered Deidre a quick hug. Winking, he patted

Patrick on the back. "I guess I should go back to my day job. Thanks for the long lunch, Claudia."

"No. Thank you!" she called as he walked out the door. Turning to Deidre, she mimed locking her lips before walking into the kitchen to start on some dishes.

"Oh, no. You are not getting out of it that easily," her friend laughed, slowly following behind her.

"For the record," Claudia said. "We did not have sex in the stock room."

Deidre laughed heartily.

"But I did think about it."

"I knew it!" Deidre exclaimed, thrusting her fist into the air. "I knew you two would be good together."

"I don't know about all of that, but I do enjoy his company. And running my hands on his naked body." She winked before changing the subject. "What did the doctor have to say?" she asked.

Deidre sighed. "If nothing happens naturally between today and tomorrow afternoon, he wants to induce. Which means that they'll use medication to start the birthing process."

"How do you feel about that?"

"I'm torn, honestly," Deidre replied, her eyes filling with tears. "I need to know that this little one is safe, and I can tell better if I can lay eyes on her. But I'm also terrified by the potential consequences of an early birth."

Claudia moved to hug her friend, despite her dish soap-covered hands, but stopped short as her mind focused on one little word. "Wait? Her?"

The tears fell down Deidre's face. She smiled and nodded. "Yes. Her. We had them tell us today."

Claudia lost all sense of keeping cool and squealed in delight. She threw her arms around Deidre. "You're going to have a baby girl?" She looked to the doorway where Patrick was leaning, smiling goofily. He nodded. Claudia ran over to hug him, too. "Well, that settles it. Now I have to go shopping. She'll need one of those 'my first camera' toys. No, we'll just go straight to a Cannon."

Patrick laughed and squeezed her shoulder. "Let's start with the toy version, Auntie Claude."

Ferrymen Sports Park

River Styx, Ohio

Saturday, April 3, this year

ELLIE HAD JUST TAKEN a short sip of water from the straw of her cup when her mother appeared on the bleachers next to her.

"Hi, Mom!" Ellie smiled warmly and moved some of Eddie's stuff out of the way so that Alice could sit down.

"Hello, my love," Alice replied. She sat and began to poke around in her purse for a few minutes before triumphantly pulling out her sunglasses. "Am I late?"

"Is that even a thing in baseball spectatorship?" She smiled. "No, they are just in the top of the second. There are two more in the lineup before Eddie."

"Where's Greg?"

Ellie pointed to her husband. He was leaning on the fence behind the home plate, his fingers laced through the squares in the wires, and his long arms stretched up, showing off his strong biceps, even through his black long-sleeved t-shirt.

"Good eye, good eye," Greg shouted encouragingly to the batter as he checked his swing at a bad pitch.

"Great, I was hoping to get you alone for a few minutes," Alice said, leaning into her daughter.

Ellie's heart froze. Could she know? Keeping a smile on her face, she mustered up a response. "What's up?"

"I'm sorry if this feels like I'm springing it on you, but honey, I'm selling the house. The agent is listing it today," Alice said.

Ellie inhaled sharply, her vital organs returning to normal functioning.

"Oh, honey, I know it's a hard thing to reconcile with, but it's just one of those milestones in life. Even if it's a sad one."

"It just seems sudden," Ellie replied, exponentially glad for the offered false narrative to her reaction. She sighed. "I'm sure you've looked at the finances on this decision. Where are you going to live?"

"Well, I'm moving into the new senior condo community just over there!" Alice confided, gesturing past the ball fields. "I'll be able to walk over for the boys' games. I won't have to worry about yard work or anything like that. It's a two-bedroom, so I can have a studio space!"

Alice studied her youngest daughter's face. Even without her perfectly winged eyeliner, long lashes, bronzy complexion, and red lipstick, Ellie was still one of the most beautiful creatures that Alice had ever seen. She may have been a bit biased, but she also knew her daughter like she knew her own soul. Under the blue RIVER STYX HIGH FERRYMAN MOM sweatshirt, there was a tightness to her daughter's posture.

"Ellie? Is there something else on your mind?" she asked.

"No," Ellie responded quickly. Alice's head tilted slightly, a sure sign that she had noted the agitation in her daughter's voice.

"Eddie's up," she added, jutting her chin out to indicate her son in the batter's box.

"Ah," Alice murmured, turning her attention to the game and her grandson. On his second swing, he popped a ball out into the center field, and the other team's outfielder was nowhere in the vicinity when it landed. Eddie ran to second base before the ball had returned to the infield players.

"Are you fighting with Greg?" Alice asked, trying again to pull out the source of her daughter's current mood.

"Mom!" Ellie scolded. "No. Greg's an angel, as always. I'm just...for one thing, I'm cold," she shrugged, stalling, and reached into her large bag to pull out a fleece blanket. "For another, I'm running through all the things that will suddenly need to be done for you to move."

"Oh honey," Alice chided back. "I've got all of that covered. I do have a handle on these things, you know! Really, who do you think was the adult when you were growing up?"

117

"Grandma," Ellie replied, smiling coyly. "Grandma was the grown-up." She offered her mother a corner of her blanket, and Alice scooted closer gratefully.

"Grandma, my derrière!" Alice retorted.

Ellie laughed, thankful to have gotten out of the hot seat of Alice's mothering.

Greg came over to the bleachers at that moment. He leaned over to gently kiss Alice on the cheek, a welcoming gesture.

"Eddie's looking good out there!" he said to his wife and mother-in-law. Sitting next to Alice, Greg adjusted his black baseball cap with the electric blue ferryman, the high school's mascot, on the brim. "*Philia*, do you have any pain medication? I'm starting to get a massive headache."

"Oh, babe!" Ellie answered empathetically. "Mom, can you hand me my purse? It's in there."

Obtaining her purse, she went straight to the pocket where she had always kept a small vial of medicine. It wasn't there. She poked around the larger pocket with no success. She searched and searched, but no pill bottle appeared. She must have dropped it in Nick's car. Thinking about Nick made her eyes tear up. She hadn't heard from him in nearly a week.

Noticing her distress, Alice leaned over and brought up her purse. She quickly produced a small bottle of Tylenol and handed it to Greg. "I've got you covered!" She smiled and produced a small plastic water bottle as well.

"Thank you," Greg said, swallowing the pills. He handed the pill bottle back to Alice before wandering over to the fence again.

"Thanks, I have no idea where my bottle could have gone," Ellie said to her mother.

"It's no problem, honey."

"Okay," Ellie returned. She stared out at the field, not watching the game. She was thinking about her last meeting with Nick when she had run out of the restaurant. The memory was slowly making her crazy. She'd tried to journal through it, to make sense of her feelings, but the fear of being found out made her burn the pages. Neither approach had helped anyway.

It suddenly occurred to her that Alice was talking. She only caught the last few words.

"...let someone sit vigil to your pain," Alice was saying.

"I'm sorry, Mom. I was thinking about the boys' upcoming week. What did you say?"

"Oh! I just said that I had met with some of the church elders about Carl's passing. And that it is good to let someone sit vigil to your pain."

Ellie wished that were an option now that she had broken her own heart. But she smiled at her mother and reached for her hand. "It really is, Mom. I'm glad you took that step."

She turned before Alice could see the tear slipping down her cheek and onto the blanket below.

The Scott House

River Styx, Ohio

Saturday, April 3, this year

WITH DINNER COMPLETE AND dishes washed, Ellie excused herself to run an errand to the craft store.

After standing in front of a wall of acrylic paint for nearly twenty minutes, she chose a soft blue color. She didn't need it for anything in particular or, in fact, at all. What she had needed was an excuse to come out to this side of town. She paid for her paint and aimed her minivan for Nick's house before she could lose her nerve.

With her heart pounding in her chest, Ellie rang the doorbell. She knew that Nick should be home. But what if?

The ornate door opened. She held her breath. Then Nick's hands were on her cheeks, pulling her in for a hungry kiss. She pushed softly into the house and shut the door. Her hands found his biceps, his hair, his trim waistline.

"I'm sorry. I'm so sorry," he murmured when their lips had finally parted. She pulled him back in with such sudden force that their front teeth bumped into each other. It didn't matter. She could finally breathe again.

"Why are you sorry? I'm the one who ran out with no explanation," she said.

He wrapped his arms around her, holding her tightly to his chest. Was that a tear she felt fall on her nose? Nick sobbed into her hair.

Ellie pulled back, thoroughly startled. "Nick?" she asked, alarmed.

"I thought I had lost you. I thought I had ruined everything," he confessed, reaching for her hands.

Searching his eyes, she ran one hand down his strong jawline. Her thumb ran over his slight beard, then his soft bottom lip. She kissed him. "No. It's just complicated," she sighed, leaning into him. "I can't stay long."

She turned and walked into the living room. A fire glowed in the two-story fireplace, its reflection flickered in the tall black windows. Ellie sat down on the sofa. She was still wearing the clothes she had to Eddie's baseball game, with her hair clipped back into a twist with an electric blue claw. She slipped off her Hoka running shoes and pulled her legs up into a crisscross position. Nick watched her, then chuckled softly.

"What?" she asked.

"How do you do that so deftly?" he responded.

She looked down at her legs. "What? This?" she laughed.

"You amaze me, is all," he replied, sitting down next to her and reaching for her hand. He raised it to his lips and kissed it gently. She turned her palm to cup his face and smiled at him.

"I didn't know I was asleep inside myself until you woke me up. I was so sure that everything was unchangeable and that all I could do was to keep living on the surface. I was convinced that everything that didn't feel right was only perception, not reality," she said softly. "But I see the potential of my life more fully now. And you were the missing piece."

"I feel the same way, Ellie. I've never wanted what my brothers have in their lives, but I understand now. You gave me that understanding." He laughed softly to himself. "Do you know that I called my brother Elijah the other day just to see how he was? And he was like, 'Who is this? My brother doesn't call just because!' This! You have done this to me, Eleanor Ophelia O'Malley Kouris." He wiggled his finger at her for emphasis.

"Well, how was he?" she responded.

Nick laughed. "Good, his youngest son is about Eddie's age and has gotten into playing the drums. We discussed how we would never have been allowed to do that in the house. It was nice. I miss them." He shook his head again. She smiled and leaned back against his soft leather sofa. It took his breath away.

"I wish I could just stay like this, here talking to you all night," she confided.

"Maybe someday," he replied.

Her heartbeat seemed to slow down as she considered the possibility. Ellie felt the thrum of desire mixing with the easy feeling of being around him. Her breath caught. She wanted nothing more than to mount him, to move her hips through all the pent-up feelings and stroke his arousal through their jeans, there on the couch in the soft glow of the firelight. She wanted his hands on her butt. To run her hands through his salt-and-pepper hair.

But she had to go home. She had responsibilities.

Nick walked her to the door, and they kissed before she returned to the lonely silence of her van.

She cycled through many thoughts on the fifteen-minute drive.

She had been so naive at age 18. She thought about Eddie, only three and a half years younger. What would she do if he wanted to get married right after high school? A few years ago, her answer would have been obvious: she'd celebrate his decision to yoke his life to an assuredly amazing partner and get excited about the grandbabies that would no doubt be coming within a few years.

Naive at just 18? Ellie laughed out loud in the stillness of the night. She was still ridiculously naive, but she was certainly coming to understand more than a few things about life. How perceptions and gender roles in the community she relied on, for instance, had stunted her maturity in relationship-building and sexual intimacy.

Real life was so much more than Barbie and Ken in the Dreamhouse. And she owed it to her sons to provide a better, more realistic model of a woman. If not for them alone, then for the partners they would look for one day, hopefully far in the future.

Greg was sitting at the counter in the kitchen when she opened the door from the garage. She hung her purse up in the mudroom and placed her shoes in the cubby under her hook.

"Hey," she offered as a greeting.

He was already in pajama pants and had traded his contacts for glasses. He had his phone out and was aimlessly scrolling through something. She peeked as she pulled a glass out of the cabinet - just Instagram.

"Hey, you. The boys are up in their room. Allegedly doing homework, but it's more likely that they're watching some forbidden show, like Spongebob Squarepants. Oh," he threw his hand dramatically up to his forehead and pretended to swoon. "The horror!"

Ellie laughed at his theatrics. It was one of her favorite things about him when he let his guard down and was the silly boy she still saw inside.

"They are more than welcome to watch Spongebob. Just not on my TV. Or within earshot of me," she responded, feigning indignance. "And what are you doing?"

"Oh, me? Nothing. Just looking at some pictures of a boat my friend from high school posted on the gram. I think that's it for me, though. I want to get out to the gym early in the morning before a client meeting." He stood and kissed her on the forehead. "Good night."

"Good night," she said to his vanishing figure. Then Ellie sighed, washed her glass by hand, and went into the living room. She was wide awake and slightly revved up from her thoughts. She picked up a book she'd been trying to read for over a year and turned back to the chapter where the heroine had finally given herself to the hero. At least she could read about someone getting some action tonight.

Caduceus Hospital - Birthing Center

Poe City Limits, Ohio

Monday, April 5, this year

IT WAS A NERVE-wracking 48 hours. But then, she was in the world. Delphi Catherine Horrigan was born 6 pounds, 2 ounces, and 18 inches long.

The next morning, Claudia stopped at the Pie Hole to hang up a sign noting the birth and that the establishment would be closed for a week. Then, she decorated the storefront windows and door with absurdly large, pink paper flowers that she and Alice had crafted for the occasion. A few of the early morning walkers stopped to shout through the glass, asking about mother and child. The majority of them inquired if Patrick had fainted during the birthing process.

Such was the beauty of a small town.

Claudia assured them that Deidre was recovering well and was settling into motherhood happily, while Patrick had not passed out.

The muscles around her mouth hurt from smiling. Last night, she had been in the waiting room with Caty, Stanton, and Patrick's dad, Michael, up from Florida, where he'd retired. Around ten thirty, Patrick had come out to announce that everything had gone perfectly.

As soon as Deidre and Delphi had been cleaned up and only one nurse remained, the excited grandparents and Claudia were brought into the birthing room.

She was a beautifully angry little one, tucked into the warmth of Deidre's chest. Claudia's hand reached for the camera in her bag. Caty, however, caught it and laced her fingers with Claudia's.

"Be here...just here, in this moment. This is yours, as much as it is any of ours. You can get behind your lens in a few minutes. But steep in this part, first," Caty recommended quietly to her, the girl she considered the second daughter of her heart. She squeezed Claudia's hand for a moment before letting go.

Claudia took a deep breath. And, contrary to character, she did as she was told.

Caty had moved to the bedside and was holding one of Deidre's hands while running her other hand through Deidre's slightly tousled hair. She watched as Stanton slid his arm around his wife's waist and leaned in to admire the beautiful features of the baby, so like his own daughter.

Delphi's angry, little infant bleats crashed against her heart. Claudia understood that primal sense of rage at having been thrust into the cold, loud, real world. She crossed her arms as if that could help give warmth to the little bundle and smiled brightly. From across the room, Patrick caught her eye and returned her smile. Michael was clapping his son on the back and pulled out several pink chocolate bars shaped like cigars from his breast pocket.

"Your mother would have loved her!" Michael announced, passing a chocolate cigar to his son. Patrick nodded, tears pooling in his eyes. His mother, Darcy Horrigan, had died from cancer when Patrick was thirteen, and Claudia knew that a significant connection to her memory came from Michael.

Unable to control the itch any longer, Claudia pulled out her Nikon and began shooting the moment, grateful for the reminder to take it in. She photographed Stanton, Michael, and Patrick being silly with the chocolate cigars. And Caty holding her first granddaughter for the first time. And so many pictures of Deidre and Delphi. Claudia even allowed Deidre to get a shot of her holding the baby.

But the majority of the photos captured Delphi during her first hours in the world.

Emotionally and physically exhausted, Claudia quietly excused herself.

The tears finally started falling as she was paying the parking fee for the hospital garage. Her heart was overflowing with joy. And before she could change her mind, she was at Spencer's front door. She hadn't texted, but her simple knock had woken Spencer. He opened the door wearing a pair of ocean blue flannel pajama pants and a souvenir t-shirt from the seaside town his family loved.

Claudia threw her arms around him, her anxious mouth meeting his. He shut the door behind her as he pulled her into his embrace. Her purse dropped from her shoulder with a thunk, but neither one noticed.

Spencer leaned in to kiss her fully, but at the last minute, he pulled his head back and studied her face instead. "Baby's good? Deidre's good?" he asked, a shadow of worry passing over his face.

"They are all doing wonderfully," she announced, fresh tears pooling in her eyes.

"Had to make sure. You had me scared for a minute," he confessed before leaning back into her kisses. Grabbing his hand, she led him up the stairs two at a time.

Tantalizingly slowly, he removed her cranberry-colored sweatshirt and her black Chuck Taylors, fumbling a little with the laces. He pulled her face to his to kiss her nose, her eyes, and the tracks of her tears before returning to the task of removing her clothes.

She arched as his tongue flickered over her nipple. A small groan of delight escaped from her throat.

She pulled off his shirt, her lips finding the succulent hollow of his neck. His sharp intake of breath made her smile slightly and emboldened; she made her way up to his earlobe. A quick nibble, a short lick, and he was ready to go.

They made love softly, a cold burn compared to the fiery fever pitch of that first time.

Claudia willingly held her arms above her head, with one of his hands keeping them in that position. She watched the sparkle of his blue eyes, bright even in the darkness of his bedroom, with each thrust. The head of his cock was rubbing her internal erogenous zones in a way she hadn't known was humanly possible. Each movement brought a new, ever-heightening gasp from her.

"Oh my god," she whispered in his ear, "it's like you were made just for me. Your cock is perfect!"

Spencer chuckled softly and sucked at her pert nipples again. He watched her intently as she succumbed to the ecstasy of his movements. Her moans spurred him on, and he, too, came.

Lying down on his side, he pulled her close - big spoon, to little spoon.

"You, Claudia O'Malley, are perfect," Spencer confessed, pulling the soft comforter up and over their bodies.

Claudia almost scoffed at the idea, but it was such a wonderful button on the night that she let it slide. Instead, she smiled, gathered her hair beneath her head, and settled into the warmth of him.

The Horrigan Home
River Styx, Ohio
Thursday, April 22, this year

CLAUDIA HAD STARTED A new toothbrush, which stayed in a soft rose-colored cup at Spencer's house. It felt like a start. Like a chance.

This morning, she had woken up in Spencer's arms. *What is this feeling?* she thought to herself. *Contentment? Possibly.*

She made them, each a travel mug of coffee doctored up with a small amount of cream and hazelnut flavoring. Spencer kissed her shoulder on his way to grab a cereal bowl out of the dishwasher. She grabbed his hand and pulled him in for a long kiss. "I've got to go," she whispered. "So I wanted the real thing."

He smiled and cupped her face in his hand. "I'm glad," he replied. "Will I see you later?"

"Can we play it by ear?"

"Of course."

She smiled and gathered her pack on her shoulder. Claudia took a deep breath as she walked out the door. The morning was crisp, but the sun felt nice. Birds chirped happily in the branches. She pulled her keys from her bag and opened her door. She drove down the familiar roads, slowing to a stop in the Youngs' driveway. She ducked into the apartment to drop off her bag and change clothes. Then she walked down the stairs, out to the sidewalk, and over to Deidre's house. She knocked lightly at the door. Patrick answered it, a tiny Delphi sleeping in his arms.

They smiled at each other, and Claudia reached out to take the sleeping babe.

"Dee's asleep upstairs," Patrick whispered. Claudia nodded. "She's got another hour before Delphi will need to nurse again."

"Go sleep," Claudia admonished. "Auntie Claude is here."

She nestled Delphi's head into her clavicle and lowered herself into the armchair. Delphi stirred slightly but settled back down quickly enough. Claudia rubbed her tiny back and enjoyed the smell of her lotioned head. She reached for her coffee, only to realize it was about five inches too far out.

"How do parents do this?" she wondered aloud as she scooted a little forward. Her hand successfully reached the desired cup, and she brought it back to her face, where she encountered a new problem. Delphi was too centered on her chest, and the warm cup was coming alarmingly close to the tender skin. She craned her neck, but it was no use. She couldn't figure out the mechanics needed to take a sip. Giving up, she managed to set her cup back down on the end table and contented herself by rubbing the soles of Delphi's tiny feet.

"It's so strange to think that my Deidre, my tiny little friend, grew you in her tummy," Claudia whispered, smiling. "When I look at your mommy, I still see a ten-year-old girl."

Dephi made a tiny snort and unearthed a defiant fist from the blanket swaddle.

"That's right, girlie-pop," Claudia whispered. "Rock on!"

"Are you encouraging rebellion in my 10-day-old daughter?" said a sleepy voice from the landing to the upstairs.

"Of course. She has to learn to fight the patriarchy earlier than we did."

Deidre rubbed her eyes and came the rest of the way into the living room. Smiling, she took the baby and settled in for a nursing session. Claudia consoled herself by finally drinking her coffee.

"What is on your agenda for today?" Deidre asked her friend.

"Well, after I get in some baby snuggles and let my bestie get some sleep, I need to go check on my mom. She's moving this afternoon, so I assume she'll need some help."

"That sounds like fun, but isn't that your sister's favorite thing to do? Overseeing all situations?"

Claudia laughed heartily, making Delphi jump. "Oops. Sorry," Claudia apologized, lowering her voice. "I have no idea what my sister is doing. I am simply going with my flow, and if we flow together-great. But I will not let her undertow upset that balance and freedom."

"You are very zen this morning. Are you stoned or something?"

"Just high on life, baby!"

Deidre's eyes lit up. "Oh! I get it. You stayed over at Spencer's house!" she said, putting an extra sing-songiness on 'Spencer.'

Claudia played coy. "I'm a lady. I won't kiss and tell."

"Since when?" Deidre cackled, her laughter causing her daughter to jump, taking her nipple with her. "Ouch! That's mommy's, sweetie."

"Touché," Claudia saluted her friend with her coffee cup.

"So...how is that going?"

"Well, the sex is great."

"What happened to not kissing and telling?"

"I didn't tell you about kissing, did I?"

"Fair. Anything beyond the bedroom?"

"That's always the sticky part for me."

"I know."

"Yeah. He's really funny and smart. He can go from dragons to cricket to world events to history without breaking stride."

"You don't have to sell me on him. Patrick and I were friends with him first," she said, smiling. "Are you building the base of a relationship or just having fun?"

"Right now, I plan to stay around here for a couple of months and then re-evaluate. I don't know what that could mean for a long-term relationship. I've never had to cross that bridge. But, I will say that if things keep up like this, I could see myself trying."

Delphi gave a small snort as Deidre raised her into a sitting position. With her thumb and pointer finger positioned under Delphi's chin, she firmly patted her back until the most unladylike burp escaped. Claudia laughed as the pair settled back in to nurse on the other side.

"Do you know what we spent the bulk of last night doing?"

Deidre raised one eyebrow.

"Playing Uno. Just Uno. For hours! And we laughed and laughed. It was…nice. It was just nice to be in the moment, enjoying the companionship. I know that I spend a lot of time in my head, and it's not healthy. I'm a work in progress."

"Oh, friend. We all are! Believe me," she replied and yawned.

"Do you want to try for another nap?"

Deidre kissed Delphi softly on the head and nodded. Claudia stood up and walked over to her friend on the couch.

"Mind if we go for a walk?" Claudia asked, lifting the baby and settling her back against her shoulder.

"Not at all. The stroller is on the back porch. There's some sleepers folded on the table, along with blankets.'

"Alright, lovey. We'll be back in a bit."

"I think I'll be right here. It's already so cozy and warm!" Deidre said, already curled up and falling back into sleep.

The Kouris Home

River Styx, Ohio

Friday, April 16, this year

💬 THESE DAYS, I have a hard time deciphering what is real. Is this real? Do you love me, or just the thought of me? Or is my life at home real? Is its realness lost in its routineness? Are Greg and I just great roommates? Do I love you? Does it matter? Is love a real thing, anyway? Why does it feel so ridiculous and crazy?

Ellie watched the little bubbles pop up on her screen, indicating that Nick was typing an answer.

💬 What has put you in a philosophical mood today?

She bit her thumbnail and thought about his question.

💬 I'm not sure. I guess I feel split in two and wondering which one of me is the real one.

💬 Darling, what if they both are? Can you not have more than one facet?

💬 What if this is all an illusion brought on by the rush of nostalgia and hormones?

💬 What if it isn't?

💬 I don't know. I don't know how to navigate any of this.

💬 You could ask for a divorce.

💬 What about the boys?

💬 Couples with children get divorced.

💬 But I don't have a job or any way to support them!

💬 You would probably get child support and maybe alimony. And, dare I say it? I'll be here to help.

💬 I can't ask that of you.

💬 You didn't ask. But you are more than your sexy curves (and wow, do I love your curves!)

💬 This feels right. You feel right.

💬 What if you have been pretending for so long that you no longer know how to be real with yourself?

💬 Tell me, how does this pan out?

💬 Like, you and I?

💬 Yes, how do you interpret the tea leaves?

💬 Well, you would ask for a divorce, for starters.
Then, well, you'll have to decide what you want. Are
you going to continue to buy into the box that your
upbringing puts you in, or do you want something
different? You need to think about what you want.

💬 I want this to be easy.

💬 That's not a real-life answer.

💬 Do you love me?

💬 I do. Christ almighty. I do.

Ellie put her phone down when she heard the brakes of
the middle school bus groaning to a halt in her cul-de-sac.
Seconds later, the front door slammed, and Jacob walked
in.

"Homework?" she asked him, as she did first thing after
school every day.

"Nah. Got it all done." He poked his head into the
refrigerator and came back with the carton of orange juice.
He poured himself a glass and put the now-empty carton
into the trash can. Then he grabbed an apple from the wire
fruit stand on the island. "I'm playing Zombie Attack with
Bobby!" he said, disappearing up the stairs to his room.

"You've got 45 minutes," she called, "until we leave for
Grams'!"

"Okay!" he shouted back before slamming his bedroom
door with a loud WHAM! Ellie shook her head and
chuckled. Not that she and Claudia had always been

library quiet, but they had certainly mastered handling a door before middle school.

What do I want? she thought. This was hard. She was trained to rarely think about what she might want. There were always babies, husbands, and mothers to pacify first. Not to mention outside obligations like church callings, athletics boosters, and the like, making it more complicated. But without all those distractions? She took a deep breath and held it. She counted to ten and let it go.

💬 I want to spend days with you by my side. I want to be amicable with Greg so that the boys don't suffer. I love him, but it's different. And I don't feel like I can force that wonky situation on a new partner. My boys will also need to see that they are the best of Greg and me, but they didn't cause this split. I want to be forgiven for falling in love with you when I had already made promises to Greg, despite who did or didn't keep them first.

💬 Those seem like reasonable wants.

💬 I see a lot of pain in those wants.

💬 Sure. But I can't operate on a heart without making an incision. Wounds hurt before they heal.

💬 Sometimes, they keep hurting.

💬 Ellie - what hurts more? Being sneaky or being honest?

💬 I know you're right.

💬 Of course, I'm right.

She rolled her eyes.

💬 I, for one, love that you are MOSTLY right on many things. I have to get ready to go to my mom's.

💬 Tell her 'hi' from me!

He teasingly texted.

💬 You know I won't!

She teased back.

Cuyahoga Valley National Park
Peninsula, Ohio

Monday, May 24, this year

"LET'S GO FOR A hike," Spencer announced one evening after they had eaten dinner in her tiny borrowed apartment.

"Okay," Claudia replied. "But I'm taking my camera."

Spencer smiled at her - his sexy boy-next-door smile that made her feel like they should stay in bed despite the beautiful evening outside.

"I wouldn't expect anything less."

"Good," she said, kissing his nose. "Let me go change and grab my gear."

He filled some water bottles and put them in an orange creamsicle-colored Jansport, along with a couple of bags of nuts, while he waited. When she returned, they set out on their adventure.

"Let's go to the National Park and hike to the falls," Claudia requested.

"That's what I was thinking! We're so similar!" he said. She smiled at him and laughed. Somehow, it had become a joke between them to punctuate every mundane coincidence with a bubbly, "We're so similar!"

She snapped a hundred or more photos of flora and fauna on their way down to the falls. As she did, Spencer amused himself by examining the layers in the rock formations surrounding the Great Falls.

"I took a course on geology in college," he offered as she pressed the shutter. "But I don't remember anything other than the term 'igneous rock.'"

She laughed.

"I'm not sure if that is what we have before us or not. Either way, the view is stunning," he continued.

"I agree on the view," she said, checking a round of photos. "And I also went to college. Igneous rock develops from volcanoes. This is sedimentary rock, mostly shale, and is a result of ancient seas and streams. Come on, Pittsburgh-boy! This is Appalachian Mountain Range 101."

"Hmm," he mused, reaching out and pulling her close to him. "Cute, talented, and smart!"

She laughed before noticing her phone's soft ringtone. She pulled it out and looked casually at the caller. She jostled it a little, showing Spencer the screen. "212, New York number. I should take this."

Spencer gave her some space to take her phone call. It was a few minutes of her hushed professional voice before Claudia turned with wide eyes.

"Yes, yes. Of course! Thank you. I'm out in the field right now, so, if you could email me all the information that would be great. You, too. Bye-bye." She ended the call and looked at him.

"That was Aimee, an agent I've worked with at *National Geographic*. They want me to be a part of their travel program. It's an amazing offer. Four months of travel equal to my typical year's salary."

"Are you thinking about taking it?"

"I already said yes. It is too good an offer to pass up."

"Ah. I see." He turned and walked down the path back the way they had come.

"Spencer? What are you thinking?"

"Me? Thanks for asking. Since you did eventually ask, I was thinking about how we've started to have this great relationship where everything is flowing nicely. And I enjoy being around you and seeing the world through your eyes. But what I'm also thinking is that you didn't even hesitate to say yes to a job that takes you not just out of town, but out of the country, for four months. And it didn't even occur to you to wait for one extra minute and spare a thought for me."

"This is my job. My career. I've worked hard to get to this level. Do you understand how few people are offered these opportunities? It's not like yours. You can throw a rock in any town and hit a public relations party planner."

"Wow."

"You know what I meant."

He snorted and shook his head. His stride increased, and she picked up her pace behind him, trying to catch up.

"Spencer. Wait. Spencer!"

He stopped so suddenly that she ran into him in her efforts to avoid the tree roots covering the path.

"I get it. I really do. But I also have feelings."

"I know. I'm sorry."

"And right now, I'm just really hurt that...I don't know. I'm just hurt."

She stood for a minute, considering his words. "I'm sorry this hurt you. I am. But we've been dating for, what, three months? You're sadly mistaken if you think that three months is enough for me to give up my independence and just chuck everything out of the window that I've worked so hard to achieve. I didn't ask you because I don't need your permission to do this or anything in my life."

He shook his head. "It's not about asking me or getting permission. It's about respecting any sense of an 'us' enough to have a conversation about it first. This is an amazing opportunity. Four months away is not a long time in the grand scheme of things. I'm really excited for you. But I can't help but feel slighted by you just taking it like that," he said, snapping his fingers. "I wish I could think of a 'PR party planner' example to relate it to, but I can't."

They hiked in silence for half a mile or so.

"That was wrong of me to call what you do party planning."

"Well, you're not entirely wrong. Just rude."

They drove back to the apartment in chilly silence. Claudia vacillated between feeling angry, hurt, and sorrowful. She watched his jaw, defined by the tightness of anger. She felt crazy at the moment, but it suddenly occurred to her that she would love to kiss down the line and caress it with her thumb.

How could I be so stupid? her mind reeled over and over. *Why does he have to be so stubborn?*

When he pulled in behind Stanton's Jeep, Spencer turned slightly in his seat to face her. "I need to cool off," was all he said.

"Okay. Same," she replied and slipped out of his car. To his credit, he didn't peel out of the driveway like she probably would have. He did, however, sit for quite a while at the stop sign at the end of the block. She stood outside in the fading near-summer light until he pulled away. Then she walked down the street to Deidre and Patrick's house.

"I messed up," she said when Deidre opened the door.

"What else is new?" Deidre laughed before noticing her friend's face. "Hey? Hey. Claude. Tell me what happened."

She led Claudia through the dining room, where Delphi was snuggled in a saucer-like object that rocked slowly back and forth. Deidre put her finger to her lips. "I just got her down. Let's go to the kitchen."

Deidre got a glass down from a cupboard and filled it with ice and water from the refrigerator. "Something to drink?" she asked.

"I'll have water. That sounds good."

"Oh, honey. There *is* something wrong with you. Go ahead. Tell Mama," she said, handing Claudia the glass of water and settling into one of the barstools under the counter. She patted the other seat encouragingly.

"I just blew it with Spencer."

"Oh, Claudia," Deidre sympathized.

"I got a call for a four-month gig, and I took it without consulting him," she said, taking a sip of water. "I don't have to consult with him!"

"No, you don't," Deidre agreed. "But if you haven't indicated that you were only here for casual dating, I can see where he might think he has a horse in the race."

For her honesty, Deidre was given the 'traitor' look by Claudia.

"That's coupling, my dear. Sometimes you are going to do the thing you need to do, but you need to have the conversation first," Deidre shrugged. "Like when Michael wanted to retire to Florida, and he offered us the bulk of the share in the Pie Hole. Obviously, Patrick and I were always going to take it, but we spent a couple of days analyzing it first."

Claudia finished her glass of water and thought about what her friend had said. "I know. But this is a big deal to me because the pay will match an entire year's worth of salary. An entire year in four months!"

"Okay, but what would it have hurt in taking an extra day to discuss the topic?"

"Ugh. I wish I hadn't come back here."

Deidre faced her friend head-on, slightly shocked by the words that had come from her mouth. "So what does that mean?"

"God. I don't know," Claudia continued. "Sometimes I just want to go back to my ignorant life. It was so much easier!"

"Was it so much easier? Was it, Claudia?"

"Yes!" she answered, her voice rising. "I didn't have to worry about anyone back home. Now all I do is worry!"

"Thanks," Deidre said, matching her friend's tone and volume.

"What? No. I didn't mean…"

"Stupid Deidre. Never left home. Never had adventures or saw the world. Just got married and nearly died trying to have a baby."

"That's not what I…" Claudia started.

"Or maybe it's not a worldly bias. Maybe River Styx is just one-dimensional. Yeah, you're out there having this full life, and we are just flat game-tokens to you. Like…like those gingerbread men pieces in Candyland. Just moving through the gameboard without you ever knowing, ever seeing, where they have been."

"Dee, I didn't…" Claudia tried again, but a cry sounded from the other room.

"Please leave. I'm really tired, and I can't think straight as it is. I just need you to go."

"Okay," she threw her hands up in a placating gesture. "Okay. I'm leaving. I'm really sorry. We should talk later."

"Claudia. Just. Go. Please."

It took everything in Claudia not to run back to the apartment. Once up the stairs and in the privacy of the apartment she flung herself onto the bed. She screamed into a pillow until her throat was torn and her voice was raspy. She had forgotten to buy more tissues, and all she could find was an old kitchen towel to dry her tears and running nose.

First Spencer, now Deidre. Maybe it was time for her to get out of River Styx before she could do any more damage. And honestly, she hadn't cried so much in her whole damned life.

Claudia's Apartment

Pittsburgh, Pennsylvania

Friday, June 11, this year

"NICK IS ATTENDING A symposium at the Children's Hospital downtown, and he asked me to come stay for the weekend. But once I got here, and we were sitting in his room, suddenly it was all too overwhelming."

"Wow," Claudia responded. "I...I don't...I, honestly, can't think of a thing to say."

She shook her head and blinked a few more times before rummaging through a box to get her sister a glass of wine.

"I know, Claudia. Believe me. I know," Eleanor responded, taking the offered glass. "Greg is an amazing man and an amazing father. I do feel so lucky to be in this unit with him. He's a saint."

"There's a huge 'but' at the end of that sentence, or you wouldn't be fucking - "

"Language, Claudia!" Eleanor automatically corrected.

Claudia stared at her sister, trying to read her face and her posture, looking for anything that would give her a clue as to what wild game Eleanor was playing. Finally, she sat down on the stool across from her sister. Their knees touched lightly as Claudia reached up to brush a caramel strand of Eleanor's hair from her eye.

"Sorry," Claudia said, taking a deep breath before continuing. "What's up at home?"

Eleanor growled, frustrated by the circumstance she had put herself in. "I'm just so flippin' tired of myself, my mind. It's all just spiral after spiral, trying to find an acceptable path forward."

"I don't know, Ellie, it doesn't seem like you have a simple way forward."

Eleanor started to tell her not to call her that, but her fight was gone. Besides, it felt strangely comforting to hear Claudia say her nickname. She sighed.

"Let me get out of my head for a minute," Ellie paused, sipping the wine. She made a slight face at the perceived vinegary nature of the drink before putting it down on the counter. "Why are you moving?"

Claudia eyed her sister skeptically. First, the unscheduled visit, then the request for an alcoholic beverage, and now asking the question about Claudia's life.

"Honestly," Ellie said. "I want to know."

"Well," Claudia began. "I have been offered a four-month opportunity to be the subject matter expert for a series of reader-facing excursions for a large magazine organization. Essentially, people pay stupid amounts of money to go on a twenty-some-day vacation with writers, photographers, anthropologists, historians, and a host of others. The one I'm supporting engages a private jet and goes to places like Easter Island and the Acropolis in Greece." She stopped and took a long pull from her glass.

"Oh! I thought you were just going to say you were moving in with Spencer Siegel," Ellie stated in the pause.

Claudia was taken aback. "Wait. What?" she asked.

It was Ellie's turn to eye her sister. "River Styx is a small town, and I do run into nosy people at the grocery store," she shrugged before picking up her glass of wine again. "What happened there?"

Claudia sat her glass down and rubbed her temples before answering. "Honestly? I don't know. This is such a great opportunity, and it is the equivalent of a year's base salary in just four months! Plus the networking possibilities…"

"But you're not moving all your stuff into a private jet. Where is that going?"

"Well, there is no reason for me to keep an apartment when I won't be here for a third of the year. So, I've sold some things on the marketplace, and everything else will go into a storage unit."

"And Spencer?" Ellie continued.

"Fuck, Ellie. You're not going to let it go? Fine. I've known Spencer for three months. That's it. Three months. And, while it's been an amazing three months, it's just that.

He doesn't owe me anything, and I don't owe him. It's not like I was going to marry him after such a short...," Claudia drifted off, realizing that had been pretty much what her sister had done with Greg all those years ago. "Anyway, I'm an adult. We both have a lifetime of decisions to contend with and, for me, some of those were part of a longer strategy. I've never stopped for a beautiful man before, and I'm not going to start now."

Claudia closed her eyes, not sure yet if she trusted her sister with her next words. "But, dear god, did I want a reason to come up so I could do so." Her breath caught in her throat. She was amazed to feel Ellie's arms slide around her. Claudia's eyes burned as the tears came quickly, spilling down, warm on her cheeks.

Ellie sighed and offered her confession. "I'm really sorry, Claude. But, hey! I'm pregnant with Nick's child."

Claudia burst out laughing.

"What?" Ellie demanded, hurt by her sister's reaction.

"You seriously always have to one-up me, don't you?" she said through the laughter, pulling her sister into a deeper embrace.

Ellie stood her ground for a moment before conceding. "Usually."

Acheron

Cadenceus Hospital - ER

Poe City Limits, Ohio

Monday, June 14, this year

THE CONSTANT RHYTHM OF mechanical beeps echoed through Claudia's skull. Unknowingly, she had begun to tap them out with her thumb on her sister's hand.

Short, short, short, long. Repeat.

If she felt it, Ellie didn't react to the tapping. Claudia checked her watch. It was just after 2:00 a.m. Around midnight, she had finally convinced both her mother and Greg to go home and rest. She couldn't even think straight. She was so tired. But she hadn't left Ellie's side, save for when the doctors had requested that she step out, since the EMTs had rolled her up into the ambulance.

"You fucking bitch," she whispered, not for the first time in the last 24 hours. "You are going to get better so we can be best friends. You are going to get better so that you can see your boys grow up."

She reached for the shreds of tissue littering her lap and blew her nose. "You have to get through this so that I am not the only one who knows about your ridiculous love child."

The tears flowed again, and she just let them. She wiped the tears and snot on the bicep of her long-sleeved shirt. Still tightly holding her sister's hand, Claudia rested her head on the crook of her elbow. Sitting there, balanced between the hospital bed and cold metal chair, she fell asleep.

A nurse came to check Ellie's vitals. Groggily, Claudia looked at her watch. It was 3:42 a.m. She'd managed to get an hour of sleep.

Stanton had been kind enough to bring Claudia some of Caty's clothing - a couple of pairs of sweats and shirts, along with some snacks, water, and a small toiletries bag. Letting go of Ellie for the moment, she took the bag into the small bathroom.

Claudia studied herself in the mirror. Her dirty, matted hair was out of her face, wrapped in a scarf. There was a slight smudge of something red along her jawline. Turning the cold water tap on, she splashed her face and wiped the sleep from her eyes. Next, she opened the toiletries bag to find toothpaste, a toothbrush, and a small stick of Dove deodorant. Sending a heartfelt thanks to Deidre's parents,

Claudia put on some of the deodorant and brushed her teeth.

When she turned the faucet off, Claudia realized that she didn't hear the whoosh of her sister's oxygen machine.

She opened the door to a flurry of activity and caught the words "hemorrhagic stroke."

Stepping out of the bathroom and into the fray, she quietly excused herself to the hallway to wait for someone to tell her what was going on.

Finally, a harried-looking nurse in maroon scrubs approached her. It may have been the one who had woken her up when checking Ellie's vitals, but Claudia couldn't remember.

"You're Eleanor's sister, right?" she asked.

"Yes," Claudia answered. "What's going on?"

"Your sister has had a stroke. We need to operate right away."

Claudia nodded. "Yes, of course. Yes."

"I can take you up to that waiting area if you'd like to grab your stuff from the room," the nurse continued. "The doctor will explain when they get her stabilized. Her husband is listed as a healthcare power of attorney; are you able to call him to come in?"

Claudia grabbed onto the bumper rails lining the wall as all of the air suddenly left her lungs. With a concerned look, the nurse reached out in case she should fall, but Claudia just waved her away.

"That sounds scary, but yes. Yes, of course, I can call Greg. Let me grab my stuff."

*   *   *   *   *

Greg was chewing on his thumb cuticle. The middle button of his pale blue shirt was in the wrong hole. He was bleary-eyed and his voice was gruff, like he hadn't slept even after leaving the hospital. Claudia couldn't blame him. Greg had returned home to two anxious teenagers.

She realized suddenly, that the majority of her relationship with Greg had been relayed through Ellie. She couldn't even think of the last time they'd had a real conversation or if they ever had.

The soft click of footsteps on the linoleum flooring of the waiting room broke into her thoughts. Claudia looked up.

"Mr. Kouris?" the man in teal scrubs addressed Greg. Greg looked over at Claudia, his eyes wide and fearful. She rose and went to sit next to him.

"Yes, sir."

"I'm Dr. Miller," he stated, taking the seat on the other side of Greg. "I'm a member of your wife's medical team. I want to apprise you of her condition at this moment. We were able to stop the bleeding, but because of the brain trauma from the stroke and her subsequent surgery, she needed to be intubated and will remain on a ventilator until she is stable. She's currently being moved to an ICU room. I know this is a lot to take in, especially at this hour, but do you have any questions?"

Greg took a deep breath and reached for Claudia's hand. She squeezed his hand encouragingly. Instead of answering, Greg simply burst into tears and buried his head in his hands.

Claudia rubbed his back and looked at Dr. Miller with her best no-nonsense look. "Ellie had a stroke, and the outcome wasn't good despite your best efforts. Now she's in a coma, with a breathing tube, and being moved to the intensive care unit? Am I correct?" Claudia inquired.

"Yes. That is correct."

Claudia nodded, still rubbing Greg's back as though he were a small child. "Can we see her?"

Dr. Miller nodded. "Yes, we can allow only two in at a time once she is set up in the room. A staff member will come get you once that happens. If you think of any questions, please feel free to have the nursing desk page me."

He rose and shook Claudia's hand. He looked sympathetically at Greg and patted his back before escaping behind the locked doors of the ICU.

Claudia's Apartment

Pittsburgh, Pennsylvania

Saturday, June 12, this year

ON FRIDAY NIGHT, ONCE dinner was complete, Ellie helped Claudia wash and repack her dishes. Afterward, they settled on the pullout sofa, where the girls spent the rest of the night talking about the real things in their lives.

Ellie asked if Claudia had ever been scared when taking photos in faraway places and was shocked to learn that the only place her sister had felt real fear had been following a natural disaster, a mudslide, in West Virginia, where the affected had shot back - with bullets, not film.

Then Ellie told Claudia all about Eddie and Jacob, their birth stories, and her hopes for their future. They talked at length about Alice and Paul.

"Why are you taking this job?" Ellie asked her suddenly. She was sitting on the floor and leaning against the couch that Claudia was lying across.

"I told you. Money."

"Care to know what I think? I think you are scared. I think you have been on the run from Mom and me for so long that you can't help yourself."

"Nuh-uh," Claudia offered as a stunning comeback.

"I'm right," Ellie continued. "I know I am. I think things were getting too real with Spencer, and you couldn't deal with it. So you snatched up the first thing that took you out of River Styx."

"Well, shows what you know," Claudia stated, as sisters everywhere have said at least once in their lives. "I also got into a fight with Deidre. So, it was time for me to go."

"Oh. Well, that changes absolutely nothing about what I said. And you know Deidre will forgive you when she cools down. She's operating on zero sleep at the moment and can't help having *all* the emotions."

"Ellie the Wise has spoken," Claudia announced.

"I'm the mother of two teenage boys, so I am very wise, thank you. I also have eyes in the back of my head."

Claudia swatted at the general vicinity of her sister, missing her completely. They laughed as they hadn't laughed since childhood.

When they finally fell asleep, heads buried close on a single pillow like children, the pink haze of Saturday's rising sun had just started to peek over the Allegheny mountains.

Claudia had planned on driving the last of her KEEP boxes back to River Styx that afternoon. She was in no hurry, and clearly, neither was her sister.

"Do you want to talk about Nick?" Claudia asked, interrupting the calm silence that had settled over their croissant sandwiches and coffee. "And maybe help me understand why you are suddenly drinking your religion's forbidden elixirs, wine and coffee?"

Ellie grimaced. "I'm hardly what we used to call a 'young woman of grace' anymore," she replied matter-of-factly. "Perhaps I'm just trying to find more simplistic sins to cover my biggest one."

"Noted, even though I'm not sure that early pregnancy is the best time to pick up alcohol or caffeine addictions. But maybe nicotine?"

Ellie stuck her tongue out at her sister and continued to take small sips of her coffee, pausing occasionally to wrinkle her nose at the bitterness.

"I think that it's my relationship with Greg that I need to talk through."

"Oh?"

"He's changed over the last few years. Not, like, 'evolved' or 'grew up' kind of changed...," She took a deep breath and closed her eyes. Releasing it slowly, she continued. "Greg is still amazingly loving to me, to the boys, to everyone he comes into contact with. He's well-respected at church and work. But, maybe five years ago now, there was a wall that came down between us. It was easy to miss at first, but then it became more and more impenetrable.

"I thought it was me. I thought that maybe he didn't find me attractive anymore, or that I'd become too much of a mother figure. So, I changed my hair, tried different perfumes and different makeup, and exercised more. He noticed the changes, and he commented on them appreciatively, but it didn't tear down that wall."

She laughed suddenly. "I even tried lingerie!"

Claudia couldn't help herself. Her eyebrow shot up quizzically, and she blurted out, "You hadn't ever worn lingerie? Like, never? Not even for yourself?"

"No! It didn't occur to me that I should...or could! I was a virgin when I got married. What did I need with it? But, it didn't work."

Claudia considered her sandwich for a minute, suddenly unwilling to bring up a thought that had occurred to her.

"We go to bed most nights holding hands. He still kisses me when fluffy snow is falling, and the world looks beautiful," Ellie continued. "But we haven't had sex in two or so years."

"Ellie!" Claudia chided. "Not that I was expecting you to try and pass this child off as Greg's - since that's a level of afternoon trash TV that I could never see you doing - but not having sex with your husband in two years is kind of a big deal!"

Setting down her coffee, Ellie buried her face in her hands.

"I know. I know. It must seem so silly and naive to you! It never occurred to me until this year that marriage is just a calculated risk taken with a person who you hope will never change. But people change - I've changed. Growth can be scary, but it is so, so necessary. When you're pregnant, your body changes, your baby changes, and you learn more about being in charge of this small life. You learn more about being in charge of your own life! How could I have known back then?"

Claudia put a hand on her sister's shoulder. She wanted to approach this as delicately as possible. "Ellie," she began. "Do you think that Greg could be gay?"

She expected her sister to sit up and slap her. At the very least, she expected to have her hand smacked away. But, instead, Claudia heard a small sound of agreement.

"Uh-huh."

Claudia handed her sister a napkin for her tears.

"I think a part of me always suspected, but - really - what did we ever learn about it growing up? At best, it was your trial from God. At worst - a reflection of your moral fortitude. And you were expected to fight through it, pray hard enough, and marry a good girl anyway. And, for my part, I was proud of these things in myself, of being the worthy bride and then mother. I have always seen them as assets. Until...," she trailed off momentarily. "It was the first time I saw the pure passion and want in Nick's eyes. That was when I knew. Greg loves me. Truly. I do not doubt that. But it's not a love that ticks all the boxes of a fulfilling partnership. He has never, in fifteen years, looked at me that way."

Inhaling deeply, Claudia started to put their trash into the takeout bag. Finally on a path of understanding with her sister, she measured her next words carefully. "Do you think that he understands it himself?"

Ellie busied her hands momentarily by helping to clean up their breakfast.

"I think," she began, "that if he does, he's packed it so far away that he can't bring himself to take it out and acknowledge it. I think he sees himself as he has been told to see himself - the protector of my virtue, now and forever." She snorted. "Wow, to borrow a classic Claudia line, this is fucked up."

"Why do you think I ditched that purity-culture shit in high school? And, Ellie! Language."

Ellie laughed. "I need to get back to the boys. When do you want to leave?"

Claudia considered the room. The boxes had been taken down to her car when she went out for breakfast. The only things left were her backpack and laptop, plus Ellie's overnight bag.

"Well, anything that is left, the building's superintendent is taking care of for me. But let's sit here a little longer and collect ourselves. Okay?" she said, squeezing her little sister's hand. "Maybe give in and admit that you're not going to be a coffee person."

"I like that idea," Ellie replied, squeezing back.

Cadenceus Hospital - ICU

Poe City Limits, Ohio

Monday, June 14, this year

GREG HADN'T BEEN MUCH help that whole morning. Alice came back to the hospital around 9:00 a.m., and Claudia was relieved of her spot in the room. But before she left, she stopped at the nurses' station.

"I want to know about...my sister said that she was in the early weeks of expecting a child. I want to know what's going on with that."

The nurse nodded and turned to the phone. "I can page the doctor for you."

Claudia reached out her hand and shook her head. "That will not be necessary. I'll ask when I come back."

She didn't remember the drive back to the Youngs' garage apartment, though she soon found herself there. She grabbed her backpack and keys and then ran up the stairs to the door. She wondered about Ellie's boys, what they were doing, what they were thinking. She had managed to learn from Greg that his mother was flying in to help with them until the situation became more stable. She felt a duty to help, but she was far too tired to offer to hang out with her nephews right now.

She locked the door behind her and put her belongings on the small kitchen table. The day was warm. Stanton had brought up a window air-conditioning unit for Claudia to use while she was there. She wandered over and studied the dials before turning it on low.

She adjusted the scarf she had on her head and climbed out of the borrowed clothes. She found a pair of boxer shorts and a tank top and put them on. She removed the cushions from the sofa and pulled out the double bed. It was still made up from the last time she had been here, so she pulled down the sheet and lay down.

But Claudia couldn't sleep. Finally, after an hour, she stopped trying. She rolled off the sofa bed and readied herself to take a shower. She turned the water to scalding, not caring that it numbed her skin. The numbness matched her mind and feelings. She wanted to call Spencer, but she didn't want to bother him. She finally broke down there in the shower stall, the water washing the tears and mucus dripping down her face and into the drain. The steam made it easier to breathe as she gasped and wheezed. When she was completely spent, she turned off the water and stepped out. She toweled off and threw on a pair of cut-off sweatpants and a short-sleeved t-shirt from a box.

After wrapping her hair in a warm towel, Claudia ventured a look out of the garage apartment's window. She noticed that the patio door to Caty and Stanton's house was open, the large screen letting a soft breeze into the family room. Before she could think twice about it, she put on some flip-flops and padded out across the driveway, through Caty's beautiful garden gate, and up to the back door. She knocked quietly. Caty appeared with a mug of tea, steaming and hot in her hands. She opened up the screen door for Claudia to come inside and wrapped her in a warm embrace.

"Your sister," Caty said, "how is she?"

Claudia just shook her head and tried not to cry.

Caty bit her bottom lip, nodding her head. "I thought about calling your mom, but I didn't want to intrude."

"Caty, honestly, I think she'd like the friendly shoulder to cry on."

She studied Claudia. "How about you? Let me get you some tea. I think I will text her that I'm thinking about her."

Caty handed her a mug with a picture of a smiling baby Delphi on it. Claudia tilted her head to look at it. The picture was one of the many that she had taken in the last few months. She smiled and took a small, appreciative sip.

"Spill the tea. Isn't that what the kids say?" Caty gave her a wry look, but the command in her voice was clear: 'tell me what is going on in your mind.'

"I know this isn't my fault, but it *feels* like my fault."

"That is hard," she replied, "go on."

Claudia cleared her throat. Caty got up and pulled a box of tissues from the pantry closet. She opened it and sat it on the table between them. Gratefully, Claudia pulled one out of the box. She dabbed her nose before returning to her story.

"She was right behind me. The light had turned green, and I took my foot off the accelerator, and she was right behind me until…there was a sound. Like a pop, but also a bang. Just a terrible sound that I can't get out of my head. I lay down upstairs in the apartment just now, and it plays over and over again. Like a terrible song that you can't clear from the cache of your memory."

Caty nodded and reached out to rub Claudia's elbow.

"I parked my car and ran back to her. She was wedged into her car, held in place by that idiot's stupid Tesla. I couldn't move her; I knew I shouldn't move her. But she was talking, and then she stopped."

Claudia turned to Caty, unable to articulate any more of the story. Her desperate attempts at breathing through the tears had turned into hiccups, which frustrated the hell out of her. Caty moved her chair closer. She reached out, laying her hand lightly on Claudia's cheek.

"Get it all out. Say what you need to say," she whispered.

"I would have done anything to trade places with her, save her boys from this hurt and fear. It should have been me." Wracked with sobs, Claudia leaned into Caty's hand. The tiny woman pulled her up from the kitchen chair and into her arms. "Why wasn't it me? It should be me."

"No," Caty replied simply. "No. This is how the river of life flows. It moves us all, branches and leaves, without premeditation. Even stones and earth are no match. You and Ellie are caught in two different currents, but to fight it, to try and bend it to your will, only builds sorrow without providing a solution."

Pulling back from the hug, she gathered Claudia's tea cup and the tissues and nudged her into the living room. She gestured to the couch, where a lone throw pillow was placed neatly in the crook of the couch's arm.

"Try to nap here. Stanton finds it a very comfortable place to fall asleep. And sometimes it's easier to fall asleep knowing you aren't alone." Caty plucked a second throw pillow from a chair and fluffed it before placing it on the couch. Then she dug through the hall closet, returning with a soft-looking, sherpa-lined blanket. Claudia obliged by laying down, and Caty covered her up. The smell of early summer honeysuckle and freshly mowed lawn wafted in through the open door.

"I'll just be in the kitchen if you need me," she whispered, but Claudia was already asleep.

She woke up to the sound of a baby toy going off. Deidre and Delphi were sitting in the middle of a pink blanket spread over the carpet of the living room.

"Sorry!" Deidre said. "Delphi is working on holding her head up when she's on her tummy. Her bear helps motivate her." Deidre pushed the button on the bear's paw again as Delphi struggled to look up at the noise from the position on her stomach.

"Deidre - " Claudia started, her still sleepy thoughts jumbled around her head.

"No," Deidre cut her off. "I'm sorry that I jumped on you when you were already down. I should have called or texted in the last two weeks, but we still have our days and nights mixed up." She yawned and then stared down at her beautiful daughter, a wistful smile creeping across her face.

"I'm sorry, too," Claudia said. She got up from her temporary bed and sat next to her best friend on the blanket, pulling her into a hug. Delphi gurgled, and the two women momentarily turned their attentions back to the baby.

"How is Ellie?" Deidre said, breaking the companionable silence.

"It's not good, Dee. Not good, at all." She reached out to let Delphi catch her finger in her tiny, chubby fist. Claudia stroked the soft skin with her thumb. "And I don't know what to do with myself. I just feel so helpless."

"You, Claudia Paige O'Malley, have always been so focused on your next steps down the path in front of you. Sometimes you just have to be still."

"Still. Like photographing a lioness? No. It's not the stillness that is hard for me. It's allowing myself to feel the multifaceted emotions I'm having. It's not something I ever learned how to do. I had more of the 'stuff it down deep and put on a smile for the menfolk' kind of upbringing. Self-examination is new for me."

"Oh, Claude. I know that. I know you. Deep down inside of that chic leather coat exterior, you are warm and gooey and you love me and Eleanor dearly." She reached over and touched her friend's hand, still entwined with her daughter's. "Mostly me, obviously."

"Obviously. And...I know that you're not one-dimensional."

"I put my own fears of smallness onto you," Deidre offered. "And that wasn't fair. But in my defense, I was really, really tired. And probably hangry. Like Little Miss

Drooly here is about to be." She swept Delphi up into her arms.

"Thank you," Claudia said.

"Always," Deidre replied.

The Youngs' Garage Apartment
River Styx, Ohio

Tuesday, June 15, this year

CLAUDIA WAS DREAMING ABOUT being outside the Treasury at the Petra complex in Jordan when the soft knock at her door broke through her dreams. She struggled to open her puffy eyes but obligingly got out of bed and shuffled to the door, thinking that it must be either Caty or Stanton coming to check on her. To her surprise, it was Spencer.

"Good morning, Claudia."

"Spencer! Good morning. Oh! Come in," she shifted in the doorway, giving him room to pass through. She glanced over at the wall clock above the window. It was almost nine in the morning.

"I'm sorry to just show up. But, well, I wanted to see if... I mean...I wanted to say...Did I wake you up?"

Claudia covered her morning-breath yawn and rubbed her eyes. "That obvious, eh?"

"Oh, Claude. I'm sorry. I'll just text you later," he said, retreating toward the door.

"No," she implored. "Please. Just give me a minute. Have a seat; I can make us some coffee after I get dressed." She pulled out a pair of jean shorts and a soft yellow tank top from her box of clothes and headed for the bathroom. When she had brushed her teeth, changed clothes, and tamed her curls into a ponytail, Claudia took a deep breath and studied herself in the mirror. She didn't look half bad for a woman whose life had taken a sudden cliff dive into a primordial hellscape.

"I wanted to see if you'd like to go to breakfast with me. The library is having an evening event today, so I don't have to be there until noon," Spencer asked as she exited the bathroom. "More importantly, perhaps, I wanted to make sure that you're eating after everything that has been going on."

Claudia gave a halfhearted smile and shrugged. "I had some peach jam straight from the jar last night. Does that count?"

Spencer shook his head but smiled. "Grab your bag. I'll drive. Pancakes are on me."

"Deal," Claudia replied, sliding her feet into a pair of deep red Converse. She locked the door as they exited and walked carefully down the stairs. "Spencer? I really appreciate you coming to check on me."

"What are friends for?" he countered. He opened the passenger door, and she slid in.

The air was thick with words unsaid. She leaned back against the seat and watched the landscape pass in a soft blur. Spencer was driving out to the edge of town, where an IHOP promised cinnamon dulce and peach toppings for pancakes. There was a chill to the morning, and Claudia wished she had grabbed a sweater.

Once seated and caffeinated, with their orders placed, Claudia tried to stifle a small shiver. Spencer noticed and excused himself for a minute. She clutched the warm mug of coffee and studied the diners seated near them. An older gentleman helped a small girl, maybe a granddaughter, cut up her pancakes while the boy beside him smothered his in syrup. Across the way, two women gossiped about grandchildren and the handsomeness of the new male nurse at the doctor's office.

When Spencer returned, he held a quarter zip jacket in his hand. He offered it to Claudia, who smiled and accepted it gratefully.

"Thanks," she said, pulling it over her head. It was soft and smelled of Spencer's cologne. Her stomach clenched at the memory of being in his arms. "So, what crazy drama has upended your life in the past few weeks?"

He chuckled appreciatively at her sarcasm. The waitress appeared with their plates and a new carafe of coffee.

For a moment, Claudia was in a mentally safe space as she busied herself with the activities of dining in a restaurant - pouring more coffee, unrolling her utensils, and putting her napkin on her lap. Those actions finished,

Claudia sighed. Looking Spencer in the eye, she started her apology.

"I'm sorry about how I handled myself when I got the call for the travel job. Until you - until us - I hadn't been in a relationship that was built on any sort of foundation. I've always put my financial independence and career first. And while I still maintain that I am an adult woman who can make decisions about her own welfare on her terms, I understand how a lack of dialogue around such decisions can rock a foundation. I'd like another chance to build something with you." She took a deep breath and waited, her fork hovering over her plate as she listened for his answer.

"I understand. And I'm sorry that I wasn't respectful of your independence. It would seem that I am more of a Neanderthal than I knew. But, Christ, Claudia, it threw me for a loop. The idea that you would just hop on a plane and leave. Because, well - what if you didn't come back?" He reached across the table and looked deeply into her eyes. "I was afraid that it meant the end. And I don't want it to be the end."

She let go of the breath she'd been holding. "I don't either. I really don't. If I'm being completely honest, I missed you deeply since that day at the park. God. I didn't even know I could miss a person this viscerally, but I do. I missed you like crazy," she said, noting how easily the tears had come and spilled over onto her cheeks.

Spencer produced a travel pack of tissues from somewhere and handed her one. "I missed talking to you every day," he confessed. "But I figured you didn't want to hear from me. Then I heard about the accident, and I needed to make sure you were okay, even if it meant you'd throw something at my head."

"I'm not a throwing kind of gal."

"That is wonderful to know," he laughed.

They settled into a comfortable rhythm of eating and chatting about little things. Spencer didn't bring up Ellie, and for that, Claudia was grateful.

Later, when he pulled up to the garage apartment, she asked if he'd like to come upstairs.

"I'd love to, honestly, but I have to go get ready for work. We're hosting a lecture series tonight, and I have a few things that need to get done before the event begins."

"So, you've planned a party?" she asked slyly.

He cocked an eyebrow at her and frowned.

"Too soon?" she teased. "My apologies."

Spencer laughed and grabbed her hand. He pulled her in close, and their lips met. She could have cried, she was so overcome by that simple movement.

"How about a party tomorrow night, just the two of us? I'll make dinner," he asked, still holding her hand. She leaned over to kiss him again before opening the car door.

"I'd be honored," she replied, letting go of his hand and slipping out of the car. She gave him a little wave as he drove off, then realized she was still wearing his jacket. Smiling to herself, she gave the collar another sniff and sighed. Buoyed by the revival of her relationship with Spencer, she started to feel less like she was drowning in the chaos of her life.

The Pie Hole

River Styx, Ohio

Wednesday, June 16, this year

CLAUDIA'S PHONE CHIRPED AS she was clearing away the dishes from Spencer's dining room table. Hitting the green answer button, her eyes registered surprise.

"Hey, Patrick. What's up?" She could hear the din of the pub in the background.

"Hi, Claude, I'm sorry to bother you with this. But, well, I've got a situation here at the Pie Hole. Any chance you're with Spencer?"

"I am."

"Great, could the two of you come down here?"

"What's going on, Patrick? Is...," she trailed off, not able to come up with a sentence that didn't go too far off the deep end into crazy.

"Hey, no. It's nothing with Dee or Delphi. There's just, well, a situation that I need your help with. But bring Spencer." He hung up before she could answer.

She relayed the message.

Spencer cocked an eyebrow. "I don't think he would call unless he needed something..."

"I know he wouldn't. Let's go see what's happening."

* * * * *

"So this is going to sound crazy," Patrick started before either Spencer or Claudia had even passed the threshold between the backdoor hallway and the dining room. "Nick Scott is here," he said, then braced for Claudia's reaction.

"I'm not surprised," she responded. Patrick's mouth dropped open.

"That wasn't what I was expecting. But okay. He wanted your phone number. He says he needs to talk to you. But like hell I'm going to give him that."

"Okay," she replied. She put her hands out, palms up. "Where is he now?"

"Wait. I'm still really weirded out by your reaction. What is going on?"

"Patrick!"

"You'll tell me later," he glanced at Spencer, who was watching the exchange like a ping-pong match. "You'll tell us later." Spencer nodded his eyebrows, still in the adorable quizzical look. She balanced on tiptoe and kissed his cheek, then gave a lightning-quick tug on Patrick's chin fuzz.

"Hey! Ow! Sorry. He's in the office. When I wouldn't give him your number, he said he'd wait here and proceeded to drown himself in coconut rum. He's quite drunk and getting rowdy, thus, your backup here," he said, nodding his head toward Spencer. "And for the record, Spencer is here to make sure you don't start a barroom brawl."

Claudia looked at Spencer and sighed. "Stay by the door. I'll let you know if I need you." She looked at Patrick again. "Coconut rum? Is he a sorority girl on a breakup bender?"

Continuing around the corner of the hall, she ducked behind the bar, pushed on the swinging door, passed through the kitchen and headed to the back of the storage room, where Patrick's office door was open. Her stomach clenched. She had no idea what she was walking into, but she didn't feel like Ellie and the baby were either Patrick's or Spencer's business. So, she had to face this alone.

"Nick."

He spun slowly in the chair and looked at her. He looked exactly like she remembered, though much grayer around the temples. His eyes were darkened, like he hadn't slept in quite some time, with a slight red rim from crying. And though his button-down shirt was rumpled, he still carried that air of righteous superiority.

"Claudia," he rasped. Then, he cleared his throat. "Do you know why I'm here?"

"I have an inkling. What I don't know is why you're bothering the Horrigans' place of business."

"Be sensible, please." Even nineteen-plus years later, this man knew exactly how to get under her skin. And he must have sensed it, too, because he put his hands up in a placating gesture. "What I mean is, it's not ethical for me to go through her file at work. I had to talk to someone, and I thought that you might give me a chance. But what I didn't know was how to get ahold of you without disturbing your mother, so my best bet was to check here. I have to know what is happening with Ellie. And I suspect you know why that is." He lowered his head into his hands. "I can't imagine what you must be thinking right now."

"I'm torn on the subject, quite frankly," she launched in, full of fire and rage - not hurt by either party so much as angry over the predicament her sister and Nick had placed her in. "I see you for what you are, a coward. On the other hand, I don't know if Greg could even begin to deal with the betrayal right now."

He jumped up, startling her, the office chair flying backward into the door with a loud bang. But he didn't seem threatening, just agitated. Still, she took a step back as he served her venom back at her.

"Want to know what I think? I think that you have some nerve, coming back here to throw this situation in my face. Oh! I knew you were fiery, but I had no idea that you were this explosive, too. A coward?" he snorted. "A coward! I love her. Genuinely. She makes me want more for myself, for us. I want to be with her, but I can't make her decisions for her. All I know to do is hold on tightly for as long as possible.

"And now! God! What if she dies? I couldn't even mourn her in any sort of public way because, to everyone else in her life, I hold no meaning. Just a footnote on an early page of her 'amazing' sister's biography."

"Do not bring me into this. We were kids when I walked away from you," she said, studying him objectively for the first time. He looked so sad. Though she was still mad as hell, she softened her voice a little. "God, Nick. Do you even care that she is pregnant?"

The color drained from his face as he fell back into the chair. She crouched down to be next to him. "You didn't know," she said, the realization suddenly hitting her. She studied his tear-streaked face again, looking for any hint that she was wrong. "Oh, Ellie. Fuck. You really didn't know?"

He shook his head slowly and opened his mouth to speak when Spencer called her name.

"Claudia?" he called questioningly, his head popping into view of the office.

"It's okay, Spencer," she replied. She looked him in the eye before adding a request that would give Nick and her more time to talk. "Hey, since you're back here, could you grab us a couple of waters, please?"

Spencer nodded slowly, eyeing her closely. She nodded reassuringly. "Water? Sure thing," he said, pushing back through the door.

"She didn't tell you? That night in Pittsburgh?" she whispered, leaning in.

"I think I need another drink," he replied, trying to get up. She held her hands out, discouraging such action.

"You need water and maybe an Uber," she offered. "I only know as much as she told me that night, which wasn't much. Since she's been in the coma, I've learned that she is about 14 weeks along."

"But...," he stammered. "Let me take this in for a minute."

"Buddy, you don't have a minute. Spencer is going to be back with those waters."

"Okay. Okay, a baby. Wow. And you're sure...?"

"That it's yours? Again, I only know that she named you and stated that you are the only partner she's had in quite some time," she studied him for a minute, chewing on a thought. She wasn't able to address it, though, as Spencer came back to the office with two glasses of water and a look that said he wasn't going anywhere without her.

She channeled her best professional attitude. "Spencer, have you ever met Dr. Nick Scott?"

"I don't believe I've had the opportunity," he replied, handing Claudia and Nick each a glass. "Nick."

"Nick and I dated way back in high school. But I understand that he's cultivated a friendship with my sister in the intervening years," she continued. Spencer's eyebrow popped up again.

"You don't say," was all he offered before moving towards Nick to help him stand. "Come on, let's go out to the dining room where we can all sit more comfortably."

Claudia gave Nick a look that clearly stated, 'We can discuss this later,' as she rose.

Patrick watched, on edge, as the three of them walked past the bar and over to a booth on the emptier side of the room.

They settled in, Nick on one side of the table with Spencer and Claudia on the other. Casually, Spencer put his arm around Claudia's shoulders. This obvious show of 'mine' was a strange power maneuver coming from him, but Claudia decided to let him have this moment. She'd address it later.

"Nick," she started, "I want you to meet Spencer Siegel. He is a good friend of Patrick and Deidre, and we've been seeing each other for a few months now." With that final pleasantry out of the way, Claudia took a long sip of her water. "So, Ellie. Her situation continues to be stable, she has been intubated and in a coma since a few hours after the car accident. There's not much more I can tell you." Nick started to speak, but she put her hand up before he finished drawing a breath. "I'm sure that you have a lot of technical questions, but I'm simply not the person to be able to answer them."

Nick spun the water glass in the pool of condensation. He chose his next words carefully. "And the accident? How did that happen?"

Claudia prided herself on being a reasonably straight shooter. She hated how much of the narrative regarding Ellie's situation was covered in deceit and how she'd had to spend the last few days stepping lightly around her mother, her brother-in-law, and now Spencer. But she was steadfast in following the line between her truths and her sister's half-truths, feeling that it wasn't her place to reveal all the subterfuge. That being said, this part of the story was hardest for her to tell.

"Well," she began, wishing she had a whiskey instead of just water. "She had come out to Pittsburgh and stayed the night at my apartment. We both left around noon, maybe closer to one, she driving her car, me driving mine. We both had boxes from my apartment. I'd turned my keys in that morning.

"We spent some of the time on the phone, just chatting. She was behind me because I always take this shortcut to avoid being on the toll road, back near Youngstown, so she was following me." She could feel the tears threatening and a tightness gripping her chest. She felt a comfort now in having Spencer's arm around her.

"It is all such a blur. The light turned green, so I went. But this car on the crossroad ran through the light and - BANG! - right into Ellie. I pulled over and ran back to her. She was still conscious, dazed - but talking. The ambulance came, her leg was broken, and then there was a blood clot, and she had a stroke. Now, she's in a medically induced coma. And that is all I know."

Spencer and Nick both studied her.

"May I please have your phone number so I can get updates on her condition? I don't want to bother poor Alice," Nick asked.

Claudia looked at him. The tears were pooling in the corners of his eyes again. She reached for the end of the booth, where the table met the wall, and pulled a napkin from the dispenser for him to use.

"Fine." She rummaged through her bag and pulled out one of her business cards. Handing it to him, she said, "I can see what Ellie's friendship means to you. And I appreciate that."

"Let me get you a ride, man," Spencer said, suddenly ending the conversation.

"No need," Nick replied, flashing his cell phone. "I've got it taken care of. I'll just go wait outside." He plucked three one-hundred dollar bills from his wallet and handed them to Claudia. "This should cover my tab and tip. Please offer my apologies to Patrick."

With that, he stood up and woozily walked toward the front door. The bell tinkled as he let himself outside into the night air.

The Pie Hole

River Styx, Ohio

Sunday, June 20, this year

"WHAT. THE FUCK. WAS that?" Patrick whispered as he slid into the booth after Nick had exited.

Claudia put her head down on the table and slid the hundred dollar bills over to him.

"Claudia. Seriously. What is happening? Because I've crafted three thousand and fourteen different scenarios in my mind over the last hour." He turned slightly, noting that a patron was approaching the bar, then stood back up, grabbing the cash. "I'm not done with you."

Spencer's eyes were on Claudia. She could feel them. "Do you want to talk about it?"

"No," came Claudia's voice echoing off the table's shiny surface.

"Okay," he exhaled. "But I can see that something more is bothering you. And you can always trust me." They sat in silence for a few minutes, Spencer studying the back of her head and the curve of her spine. Quietly, he slipped out of the booth.

"Do you remember the time that we were playing matchbox cars in your backyard, and your dad had just laid in a new concrete walkway?" Patrick's voice interrupted her thoughts. She pulled her head up, dazed, and her mind racing.

"Maybe?" she replied.

"Well, we decided that it was cured enough for us to drive our cars on it, right?"

"Okay, this sounds more familiar."

"But it wasn't ready. And we ended up making little matchbox tire-sized grooves in the new sidewalk. Which was pretty cool, but you had this weird sixth sense that Ellie was going to figure it out and tell on us. So we ditched the cars by sinking them in the sidewalk right before your dad came out with Ellie trailing behind."

"And you," she said, picking up the story, "you were like, 'They just drove in by themselves!'" She laughed. "I'd nearly forgotten. But, Patrick, I do not see your point. What does that have to do with any of this?"

"How did the confrontation with your father turn out?"

"Um," she thought for a minute. "He talked to us about what we were doing, fished out the cars, and made us a wooden map to drive on. But I don't remember getting in trouble."

"We didn't. And I've thought about that a lot as I've approached fatherhood. He asked about our curiosity. He engaged in the fun. But he never scolded or berated us. And he made a point to include Ellie in it. Claude, I shouldn't have come at you like I did. I just want to see things from your perspective and help you and Ellie with whatever is going on here."

"Thank you. I really appreciate it. And if I felt like I could spill it, believe me, I would, but I'll say this. Ellie has an SUV-sized "matchbox car" in the concrete mess on her hands when she wakes up. And I'm afraid that Dr. Nick Scott has a part to play in the clean-up."

"Well, he's still a pompous dickwad, but he tips well, so I'll leave it at that. Can I get you anything?"

Claudia thought for a minute. "Do you have any of that peanut butter pie, like your mom used to make?"

"I do. Peanut butter pie and a bourbon? Coming right up."

She pulled out her phone as she waited and saw that she had 12 texts. One was from her mother, one from Greg, and the rest from Deidre.

Given the large number, she clicked on Deidre's first.

Patrick says Nick Sc

ott is at the PieHole? What's that about?

Why does he need your number…what's

going

o

n?

💬 OK, breastfeeding a wiggly baby and texting are not

💬 easy! Ugh.

💬 skdkdfjowo

💬 Just call me when you can, please?

Claudia snorted and laughed out loud, so loud that the table two over from hers turned around. She gave them a hurried smile as Spencer slid back into the booth with two pieces of pie and two bourbons.

"Thank you," she said, taking the offered fork from his hands.

"Anytime," he replied. She smiled at him wistfully. Everything in her life felt so topsy-turvy that she was having a hard time focusing on putting one foot in front of the other with any steadiness. And though she was sure that Spencer understood her predicament, she wasn't used to being directly engaged in social dynamics. Perhaps, she was now realizing, she simply wasn't used to paying attention to anyone other than herself. Maybe her "self-sustaining fortitude" was just "egotism."

Dipping her fork into the pie, she took the first blissful bite, groaning in appreciation. "Patrick's mom, Darcy, would make me this pie every year for my birthday - the whole pie just for me. But more importantly, she'd send me a few slices when it was time for my period almost every month," she laughed at the memory. Spencer blushed slightly, and she laughed more. "Sorry, but it's true."

She glanced back at her phone. Alice had texted an update on Ellie's condition. She checked the next text.

Strangely, it was Greg who asked if she could meet for coffee in the morning.

💬 Of course, she quickly texted back. Then, she gave her mother's message a thumbs up to show she'd read it.

She took another bite of pie and washed it down with a quick swig of the bourbon. The two flavors chased each other around her tongue as she carefully measured her next words.

"So, I do have one thing we need to clear up," she said, turning on a business-like air. "What was up with the possessive arm thing when we were talking to Nick?"

"I told you. I'm learning that I'm more of a Neanderthal than I'd like to admit," he confessed, shrugging. "I was a little intimidated by the cardiac surgeon ex-boyfriend getting drunk on a Wednesday night because he can't get your phone number."

She speared a forkful of pie and waved it casually as she spoke. "That's fair. Would it make you feel better if I told you that every time he speaks, I want to throat-punch him?"

Playfully, Spencer grabbed her hand and took the bite from her fork before answering. "Mmmm. Yes. That does make me feel better," he smiled at her through his stolen bite of pie. His beautiful eyes sparkled.

"Let's take the rest of this to go?" Claudia stage whispered.

"That makes me feel even better."

Caduceus Hospital - Cafeteria
Poe City Limits, Ohio
Thursday, June 17, this year

GREG HAD BEEN NURSING a Diet Coke when Claudia walked into the cafeteria. He hadn't shaved in days, but he smiled reassuringly as she took a seat across from him.

"How are the boys?" she asked.

He took a deep breath before answering. "They're fine. My mother is here. She's taking care of them. She rarely gets so much solo time with them, so she's spoiling them rotten while she can. I think that today she was taking them to the waterpark in Columbus."

Claudia smiled. "That's good. That's really good. And how are you?"

Greg looked at his cup for a full minute before dropping his face into his hands. "Claudia," he said, "I don't know what to do with myself. I am terrified of losing her. But the reason I called you is much more complicated than just her being in a coma right now."

Claudia braced herself. *He's got to know,* she thought. *Surely, by now, he must know about the baby. And that it's obviously not his.*

He pulled a handkerchief out of his back pocket - such an old-fashioned gesture, but spot on for what Claudia knew of him. He wiped his eyes and blew his nose before he began. "Ellie is pregnant. She's 14 weeks along. I don't know if she confided in you or not."

She reached across the table and took his hands. Claudia measured her words carefully. Looking him in the eye, she began. "I'm sure you know that my sister and I have not been the best of friends for a very, very long time. But that night she came to my apartment in Pittsburgh. We had the most cathartic talk that we've ever had. She told me some things that I've been thinking aren't mine to tell. And I just hope that she wakes up so that I don't have to be the one who...," she trailed off.

He nodded, seeming to understand what she was saying. Claudia watched him screw up all his courage to ask his next questions. "Was my wife having an affair? Do you know whose child that is? Because it's not mine, and I can't help but feel a little relieved by that."

Claudia didn't know how to respond. This certainly wasn't the way she expected it to go down. She opened and closed her mouth several times before admitting to herself that she didn't know what to say. Greg leaned close across the table.

"Claudia. I would never hurt your sister for anything. But I've come to realize something about myself in the last few years. For a multitude of reasons, I didn't want to admit it to myself. But then I found out that she was carrying a new life, and I was relieved! But, also, I knew that I couldn't go back to pushing the truth away."

"I wish I knew what to say to you, Greg. I wish I knew how to make that heartbreak evaporate, but I don't. Though I am happy to listen to you, without judgmental hang-ups, if you need a safe space to talk through things."

He studied her as he wiped the tears from his eyes. "I love your sister deeply, but I don't love her as a man should love a woman. I don't know that I was ever fully capable of doing that. But we have two amazing boys, and she curates this amazing and fun life for us. I love these things about her. I had hoped that was enough, but now I see that wasn't fair to her. I wasn't fair to myself. If she pulls through this, I will do anything she wants. Despite all of this, she is my best friend, and I can't lose her."

Claudia was crying. She reached into her backpack to find a tissue and cursed softly when the only thing her hand came back with was an empty sleeve that had once held tissues. Greg handed his handkerchief to her, and she gratefully - if slightly grossed out - took it to blow her nose and blot her wet cheeks.

"Do you think this makes me a terrible person?"

"Oh, Greg. No. No! I think life is just Newton's third law, the one about every action having an equal and opposite reaction. Our parents and their generation were blinded to the true human condition and did us a disservice by teaching us about morality and ethics in the dark. The more I experience the flow of life through other cultures and spaces, the more I am aware of this fact. You don't have to hold yourself to their teachings anymore. You simply came to understand who you were after you had made some big life decisions. Ellie made decisions based on how your actions affected her sense of self. Neither of you are terrible people. You are just people."

Despite her tears, Claudia changed seats to be next to him. She hugged him intensely. She hugged him because they both needed it. He melted into her as a child would and sobbed. She rubbed his back and shushed him like her mother used to do for her when she'd had a nightmare. Her tears fell down her cheeks and onto his head, but he didn't notice. Greg had held all this inside for a long time and was relieved to let it all out.

His feelings exorcised for the moment, he took her hand in both of his. "I'm very glad to have you here, Claudia. Though I am sorry that this is the catalyst for us learning more about one another."

"Me, too, Greg." She smiled at him wistfully before returning to her side of the table and her long-abandoned to-go cup of coffee. She took a sip to steady herself.

Both of their phones chirped. Alice.

She looked at the message, then looked at Greg. His hand was over his mouth, so she couldn't read his expression. But Alice's message was hopeful.

💬 She's starting to wake up.

Cadeuceus Hospital - ICU

Poe City Limits, Ohio

Sunday, June 20, this year

CLAUDIA WAS COMPLETELY LOST, but Greg seemed to know the path by heart.

They caught the orange elevator up to the ICU unit, where Alice was waiting for them.

"The doctors are in with her now," Alice began, tears rolling down her cheeks. "They said that this is promising, but to take it one minute at a time. When waking from a coma, there will be several stages she will pass through.

Um, I think they said she was currently in a 'minimally conscious state.'"

She reached out with one arm and pulled her eldest daughter in for a close hug. Her other hand slipped into Greg's. She took a deep, long breath and held it for a few minutes.

"It happened so fast. I was responding to a text, and I noticed that she was scratching at the tape around her IV. I told her, 'Honey! Don't scratch at that, let me get you some lotion for the itch.' And then it occurred to me that what she was doing wasn't normal for the state she was in. So I called in the nurse."

"Can we go in?" Greg asked.

"Yes, you go on ahead. We'll wait out here. There are enough people in the room without us confusing the issue." She nodded at Claudia, who was still standing in the crook of her mother's arm. It was Alice's patented 'no argument allowed' voice, which Claudia knew enough to obey.

Once Greg had disappeared into the room, Alice studied her child. "How are you? Are you doing okay? Caty texted me several times. She was worried that you were still blaming yourself."

Claudia exhaled a breath she didn't know she'd been holding. Alice took that as an answer."Don't. This isn't your fault. It's that dumb-ass man with that crazy vehicle."

"Mom!" Claudia exclaimed, shocked by her mother's words.

"He tried to kill my baby. If anything deserves swearing, that is it. Seriously though, Claudia. This is not your fault."

As they spoke, they had been walking down the long hallway. They came to a small waiting room with a couple of vending machines. Alice stopped in front of the beverage one and used her phone to pay for a Diet Coke. She looked back at Claudia, who was shocked by her mother's grasp of technology.

"What? I know how to do things."

"Mom, I'm not one hundred percent that I could figure that out."

"Oh? Well. Hmm," Alice replied nonchalantly, waving at the waiting machine. "Still a Sprite girl?"

"I think I need something a little stronger." Claudia reached out and selected the Cherry Coke button. Though she was prepared for the thud of the can dropping, it still startled her. She jumped slightly before she reached down to pull out her drink. She popped it open as Alice motioned to two of the chairs in the little alcove.

Alice's eyes were searching now. Claudia felt transported to her childhood and any time she had been less than honest with her mother.

"What is it, love? I can see that something is tearing you up. Let me carry it with you."

Claudia closed her eyes and sighed. She took a sip of the Cherry Coke, the fizzy bubbles tickling her mouth. She savored the feeling before trusting the truth with her mother.

"Mom, Ellie told me some things that I am having a lot of trouble with right now. And just now, Greg said some things that play into that. And I'm frustrated to be in the middle of this drama that I didn't seek out." Claudia hadn't ever been a smoker, save for a month-long shoot in Indonesia, but she suddenly wished for a cigarette to punctuate her words. She settled for popping the tab off of the top of the can cleanly.

"I have rarely sought out the drama I've ended up in, but there I am every time, paying the band and the stagehands. Does that mean you know about the baby? What can you share?"

Tired of all the secrets, Claudia told her mother everything from Ellie's affair to Greg's confession and the truth of the baby's paternity.

Alice, to her credit, simply took it in. She nodded sagely in all the right places. When Claudia was done, Alice spent a few minutes considering her Diet Coke.

"I knew something was going on with Ellie. But I was enveloped in my own life - Carl's death and selling the house. And she wasn't ready to talk to me, so I didn't press. But, wow, Nick? How do you feel about that?"

Claudia waved her hand. "That's water under the bridge. I certainly don't want him. In fact, I can confirm with full certainty that he still makes me want to strangle him."

Alice laughed. "I thought we were going to have to invest in a boxing ring for you two."

"Probably would have been more productive. But no, honestly, no. We were two children playing at being adults. And the farthest we ever got was a little tongue action."

"I suppose that's pretty tame, given what you've just told me about Ellie," Alice laughed. "But really, those are things better not said between mothers and daughters.

"Maybe that is precisely who those stories are for," Claudia mused.

"You may be right," Alice confessed. She reached over and patted Claudia's hand. "Let's go see what's going on in your sister's room."

They stood up, a new sense of understanding between them, and returned the way they had come. When they got to Ellie's room, Greg was alone. He was holding onto her left hand. Her wedding rings had been removed at some point, and he rubbed the white space on her tanned hand.

"She has been moving her legs a lot," he told the two women as they entered. "They said she can probably hear us, that she might even understand."

"Great!" Claudia said, stepping behind Greg to hang over the top of her sister's bed. "Eleanor Ophelia, I am so mad at you."

That got a laugh out of him. "She doesn't have to talk for me to know that she'd be saying, 'What else is new?'" He leaned over and kissed Ellie's hand. Claudia put a hand on his shoulder.

"I told Mom what we talked about," she confessed. "She knows everything that I do."

He nodded, changing his gaze to Alice. She smiled at him and stepped in to hug him. "Honey, I will always love you. Without you, I wouldn't have my boys. You will always be my son."

Greg grasped her hand as her hug ended. He kissed it, like he had his wife's, and nodded.

"Ellie, we're all here having a sob-fest. You're missing all the fun," Claudia quipped to break the tension. "Feel free to wake up anytime soon!"

Caduceus Hospital - Cafeteria
Poe City Limits, Ohio
Monday, June 21, this year

"THE CAFETERIA WORKERS ARE going to start talking about me, meeting with different men in here all the time."

"Oh, I'm sure they've already noticed, Claudia. They notice everything," Nick said, smiling and waving to the Jersey-banged cashier staring straight at them. She smiled and waved back before turning back around to her register.

"I'm just thankful I found the oat milk this time."

"Claudia. You're rambling."

Do not punch him here, at his place of employment, she reminded herself. Instead, she soothed herself by screwing up her face and giving him a hard stare. "I wanted to update you on Ellie, and I felt that meeting in person would be easier," she replied, reaching into her shorts pockets to try to find the paper she had written her notes on.

"I appreciate that, Claudia. Truly," he responded as her hand emerged triumphantly, clutching a crumpled napkin.

"No one had real paper," she answered his raised eyebrow's unspoken question. "I made do."

"Didn't say a word," Nick responded, his hands raised in surrender. Claudia made a sour face again.

"Ellie is waking up from her coma. She is currently in the 'confusional state'?" He nodded encouragingly, so she continued. "She was agitated and seemed convinced it was a school day. So she kept saying that she had to get up and get the boys to school. She eventually calmed down, but only Greg and Mom are in her room as a precaution. She's been able to eat and drink a little bit. So that's good."

"What about the baby?" Nick asked quietly.

"That seems to be progressing well. I have additional news on that front." She paused to take a sip from her to-go cup. "I've discussed the predicament with Greg and my mother. And they would like to invite you to the circle of trust. I'm honestly not sure how it has come to pass, but Greg understands that he had as big of a role as anyone in this soap opera and only wants what is best for Ellie at this point."

She watched Nick's face as he cycled through emotions: hope, stress, terror, relief. He rubbed his temples for quite a while until Claudia realized he was crying. She gave him a moment before continuing.

"Mom and Greg are upstairs with Ellie. They told me to tell you to go on up. But, Nick. If I hear anything negative about your interactions with Greg, I will find you, and you will not like it when I do."

"Thank you, Claudia. Thank you for bearing this weight, and I'm sorry it all came down to you. I want you to know that and that I love your sister very much."

Touched, she reached over and squeezed his shoulder. Then she got up, waved at the cashier, who was staring at them again, and walked out of the cafeteria.

Ellie was awake and had the potential for a full recovery. And she, Claudia, was finally free from carrying everyone else's burdens.

As she exited the hospital, Claudia noticed a Pacific-blue SUV near the curb. She ducked her head slightly and saw Spencer motioning for her from the driver's seat. She ran to the vehicle. Throwing open the passenger's side door, she leaned in and excitedly pulled Spencer into a kiss. His lips were sweeter than honey, and she couldn't help but take a quick nibble. For his part, Spencer put his hand against her face and kept the kiss going.

"I should sit outside of the hospital more often!" Spencer laughed when they finally parted. She responded by slapping him playfully on the shoulder.

"I don't care if my car is parked here forever, just take me anywhere you want right now," she asked him dramatically, pulling her legs and backpack into the seat and closing the door.

"Anywhere I want? I can think of a couple of places that seem appropriate for a party planner playing hooky."

"Fabulous. Drive on."

They talked about Ellie's progress as he drove, and that led to Claudia telling him the full story of Ellie, Greg, and Nick. She hadn't realized when he'd driven past his house, but as they reached the old part of town, she became curious.

"So, where are we going?" she asked.

"The ice cream stand has banana custard today, and I'm told that it is not to be missed. So I thought we'd go there."

"Oh, yum. I haven't had that since, well, since high school! I approve of your choice, sir."

He laughed and reached for her hand. She took his hand gratefully, a feeling of contentment welling up inside of her.

They pulled into the stand's parking lot. It was shockingly busy on a Tuesday afternoon. After they had ordered and received their large banana cones, they walked to an old bench at the edge of the parking lot, away from the other tables.

"So, Ellie is pregnant," Spencer said, taking a few minutes to process the news. "And Greg is gay?" He licked at his cone, managing to get a blob on his nose. Claudia laughed and wiped it off with her napkin.

"Yes."

"And the reason Nick was all bent out of shape the other night was actually over her?"

"Yes."

"And I assume I'm sworn to secrecy on these facts?"

"I honestly don't even care anymore. But yes, for now, you probably should be. But I have a solution for that. Let's just hole up in your house until the whole thing blows over!"

"As wonderful as that sounds, and I do mean wonderful, I don't think that will work well. I have to go to work sometime."

Claudia snapped her fingers. "I wanted to talk to you about that. I spoke with Aimee at *National Geographic* again. Given everything that was going on, I didn't want to commit to something I couldn't follow through on, but they were willing to put the offer on hold until I knew more about my sister. So I can still make their July dates, but I wanted to run it by you first." She took the reprieve to catch up on licking the drips of her ice cream, knowing that he was following every flick of her tongue.

"I...well...," he cleared his throat. "As I said before, four months isn't a long time, and this is a great opportunity, right?"

"It is. And I can keep tabs on Ellie's progress by FaceTiming with you every night until I come home after Halloween."

"Oh? Is that your plan?" he murmured.

She nodded.

"Then I think you should take it. And I appreciate you having this conversation with me."

Claudia leaned over and kissed him. He pulled her up to a standing position as she finished off her cone. They walked back to his car, hand in hand.

She watched him put the SUV into reverse before reaching her hand over to his thigh. He smiled when it made contact and put his own on top of it. Slowly she began inching her hand down into the valley between his legs.

"Oh," he said and returned his hand to the steering wheel. "I like where you're going with this. Carry on."

She did, massaging and rubbing his growing erection through his khakis. She kept her eyes trained between him, his enjoyment, and the road. It was a short drive back to his house, and by the time they got there, his cock was hard and ready. He pulled into the driveway and clicked the button to shut the garage door. Before he could reach for the door, though, she had shifted in her seat, giving herself better maneuverability to work around the center console. She kissed his lips before trailing off down his throat, while her hands worked at his belt, button, and fly.

She leaned down and, like the ice cream cone a few minutes before, licked his cock, starting with the soft foreskin. She finished the job, and he found his voice again.

"Please, stay forever."

"Careful what you wish for," she replied saucily, laughing at his contented delight.

The Pie Hole

River Styx, Ohio

Thursday, November 25, this year

DELPHI WAS SITTING IN her high chair, watching the adults bustling around her. Ellie laughed, imagining the scene through her eyes. She rubbed her growing stomach. She felt doubly awkward these days, though she knew that she hadn't yet reached the final swollen days of her pregnancy. With intense physical therapy, she had regained her ability to walk, though she'd regressed from using a cane to her walker in the last week, owing to her pregnancy gait throwing her off-balance. Luckily, the Pie

Hole had accessible entrances and areas wide enough to accommodate her wheels.

Deidre brought her a glass of sparkling grape juice and tapped her own lightly to it in a toast.

"To survival," she smiled and rubbed Ellie's shoulder.

The Horrigans, as they did every year, had closed the Pie Hole for Thanksgiving. Tuesday was the kitchen's busiest day of the year, with all hands on deck to help with baking the nearly 450 pies that had been ordered. Even Claudia had dropped by to bake a few, finding the experience extremely out of her comfort zone. Wednesday was the busiest day of the year for the bar, so Deidre and Patrick were exhausted but thankful for the amazing work done by their team.

"To thriving in survival," Ellie responded, returning Deidre's smile.

Jacob and Eddie were learning how to work the soda gun behind the bar. Patrick had trusted them to make their own Shirley Temples with as many cherries as they wanted. She caught Eddie's eye and smiled. He offered a little wave.

Michael, Patrick's father, was up from Florida and was proudly holding court in the kitchen with the older adults, the 'Grandparent Crew', as Alice, Michael, Caty, and Stanton were now referring to themselves. A cheer went up from the group as Michael finished carving the turkey and carried it out to the dining room, where Greg and Spencer had pushed together some of the 4-person tables to form one long table for all the food that the guests and hosts had prepared.

Somehow, over the din of the room, she heard a soft click.

"Claudia, come on. No pictures of me, please," she chided her sister.

"Request denied. I make everything look good," Claudia returned, sliding into a chair next to her sister and turning the camera's screen for Ellie to see. In the image, Ellie's very pregnant self seemed relaxed and happy. A faint smile played in the corner of her mouth while her soft white sweater and yam-colored scarf accented her flawless tawny skin.

"Fine, I look amazing," Ellie admitted. Claudia laughed.

"You always look amazing to me," she stated and threw her arms around Ellie.

Ellie held on to her sister's hug. She was working hard to remember to give herself grace. A tear slid down her cheek. Claudia reached to wipe it away, knocking into her sister's ruby-colored glasses, another lingering symptom from the coma, in the effort.

"Hey, oh! Sorry!" she said as she helped Ellie straighten her glasses. "I'm with you that this year can go back to the dumpster fire it emerged from, but look at where we are in this very moment."

Ellie reassessed the room. Her boys, her mother, her sister, and a team of friends who had proved they had her back were all gathered for the holiday. She was alive. They, she, and the baby girl growing inside of her, were alive. She felt the dam inside of her heart break and the tears fell freely.

"Oh, no, no, no, no. Dee! Help! I broke my sister!" Claudia called teasingly to her friend. Deidre came over and joined the hug. She had grabbed some tissues off of the bar on her way and passed them out between the other two girls. Delphi watched them from her chair before stealthily pushing her toy keys off the tray and giving them her best 'pick them up' face. The three women laughed.

During the four months while Claudia was away, Deidre and Ellie had bonded. In fact, Ellie was now doing some light bookkeeping for the Pie Hole as she made more and more strides in her recovery from the stroke and the coma, and hoped to be able to take over from Deidre in a few months.

Ellie looked up as Patrick gave a sharp whistle.

"We've got all the food out, buffet style. Feel free to grab a plate and start eating!" he called to the gathered friends and family.

Greg sauntered up. Ellie continued to appreciate his physique and the way he wore clothes cut perfectly to his frame, though it no longer set her on fire to watch him. He reached out his hand.

"You tell me what you want, and I'll pile it on the plate for you. Take my arm. It will be easier than your walker, *zoi mu*," he said.

"Thank you," she whispered gratefully. They moved at a slow pace, but he piled her oval plate high with all the delicious food and returned her to her seat by Delphi.

Michael, who was standing by Alice in the corner closest to the kitchen, leaned over to quietly ask her a question.

"How is that working out?" he asked, motioning toward Greg and Ellie.

She considered the two for a moment before answering. "The beginning was hard. Greg was a whirlwind of emotions, obviously - anger and relief. Ellie, too. So far, their adoration for each other is winning out - which is good for the boys," Alice paused and bowed her head. "I take some of the blame since I encouraged this 'marriage is forever and equals fulfillment' mindset in her. But I just want her - both, really, since Greg is like one of my own - to feel content and complete in their genuine selves."

Michael nodded. "I think Paul would be proud of them. And you," he smiled at her. She returned his smile.

Spencer, Eddie, and Jacob joined Ellie at her table. The boys had started volunteering at the library on Saturday mornings. They loved to tell anyone who would listen about the photographs taken by their Aunt Claude and how Spencer was 'pretty much their uncle.'

While they hadn't taken any steps toward marriage, Spencer had surprised Claudia with a key to his house when he had picked her up at the airport for the last time three weeks ago. She had been thrilled to say yes to the keyring.

As for Ellie's living situation, after a difficult discussion with Greg, followed by an even more difficult discussion with Greg and Nick, they had decided that the best thing, for now, was for her to move into Nick's first-floor guest suite. It was the only solution to meet her mobility needs at the moment.

Surprisingly, Nick was doing quite well at settling into a blended family life. He'd set up a room for the boys even before Ellie was out of the rehab facility in late August. They stayed every weekend and often hitched a ride with Alice to visit on many weekdays.

The back door slammed open, shocking the partygoers. Nick emerged from the hallway, freshly showered following his rounds at the hospital.

"Sorry, everyone! It's getting windy out there!" he offered, hanging his gray peacoat on one of the hooks in the hall and walking up to Ellie. He leaned over to kiss her, then put his hand on her stomach, where the baby often kicked.

"Playing soccer today?" he asked her. "I can't wait for her to be the first woman on the Arsenal football team."

Ellie smiled, pulling him down and into another kiss. It felt incredibly awkward, but it wouldn't feel that way forever. She and Greg had started divorce proceedings, and someday, Ellie knew, he would find a perfect partner to share in this life.

Claudia had once shared the thought with her that, up until this year, only death or a miracle would get her back to River Styx. In a strange twist, Ellie had proven that miracles aren't that hard to come by these days. And for that, they were both thankful.

List of Characters

- **Claudia [Claude] O'Malley** is an award-winning photographer who has spent nearly 20 years on the run from her family and her small town roots. She rejected the religious purity culture of her youth and everything her mother and sister hold dear. She's returned home for a funeral, but decides to stay for a little bit to meet her best friends' new baby, and maybe to be more-than-friends with the new man in town.

- **Eleanor [Ellie] O'Malley Kouris** is Claudia's picture-perfect sister, and she's living a double life. The quintessential stay-at-home mom, Ellie spends her days cleaning her beautiful home, raising her two boys, and trying to make her husband happy. That is, when she isn't engaging in an affair with her high school crush (who just happens to be Claudia's high school ex.)

- **Gregory [Greg] Kouris** is Ellie's husband of nearly 17 years. An East Coast transplant, he seemed so accomplished and worldly to 18-year-old Ellie, and they married later that year. They have two sons, both of whom favor their father's Grecian good looks. But Greg has secrets of his own.

- **Spencer Siegel** moved to River Styx to work as the Communications Director for the public library system. His bright blue eyes are intriguing enough to make Claudia think about sticking around to find out more about him.

- **Dr. Nicklaus [Nick] Scott** is a Cardiothoracic Surgeon, a bit of a workaholic, and Claudia's high school boyfriend. After bumping into Ellie at his office, they begin a passionate affair. Having never married, Nick is a bit of a rebel in his own right, as he and his five brothers had grown up with the same beliefs as the O'Malley girls.

- **Deidre Young-Horrigan** is 30-odd weeks pregnant with her first child and Claudia's lifelong best friend. Deidre's family and home have always been a safe space for Claudia, who needed mother- and sister- figures that didn't try to push her into one-size-fits-all life. Deidre, along with her husband Patrick, runs a popular local establishment, the Pub N' Pie (known more commonly as the Pie Hole).

- **Patrick Horrigan** is one of Claudia's dearest friends and grew up alongside the O'Malley girls. He married his childhood sweetheart, Deidre Young, and together they own his family's restaurant, the Pie Hole.

- **Alice Walker O'Malley Phillips** is Claudia and Ellie's mom. A prolific painter, she taught art before retiring. Alice is the widow of two husbands - Paul O'Malley, who died when the girls were still in school, and Carl Phillips. She has been a strict enforcer of an upright and moral way of life, but is secretly starting to see faults with that belief system.

- **Edward [Eddie] Kouris** is Ellie and Greg's fifteen-year-old son. He plays baseball for the River Styx High School Ferrymen and is pretty good at it.
- **Jacob Kouris** is Ellie and Greg's thirteen-year-old son.
- **Catherine [Caty] Yu Young** is Deidre's mother and considers Claudia a "second daughter of her heart." She and her husband, Stanton, emigrated from Taiwan before Deidre was born.
- **Stanton Young** is Deidre's father. Like his wife, he is very close to Claudia and considers her a second daughter.
- **Michael Horrigan** is Patrick's father and the former owner of the Pub N' Pie. He was best friends with Paul O'Malley. When Michael's wife Darcy died from cancer, the O'Malleys often provided a sense of respite for the widowed father, as Patrick was only thirteen-years-old. Michael later sold the business to Patrick and Deidre and retired to Florida.
- **Paul O'Malley** is Claudia and Ellie's late father and Alice's late husband. He was a teacher and an Atlanta Braves baseball fan. He passed away when the girls were in school.

About the Author

Marnie Falconer works hard to seamlessly blend her extensive experience in the nonprofit sector with a strong commitment to journalistic integrity. A lifelong resident of Northeast Ohio, she earned Bachelor's degrees in both English and History, complemented by a Master's degree in Training and Development. This academic background enables her to combine storytelling with strategic communication, creating narratives that resonate in both professional and creative realms.

From a young age, Marnie was captivated by the world of books. She distinctly remembers sitting in a little red rocking chair by her window, a copy of Little House on the Prairie in hand, carefully sounding out each word. This vivid memory sparked her enduring passion for literature and storytelling, which she channels into her professional endeavors.

Outside of her career, Marnie enjoys family life with her husband, two energetic children, and the world's most obedient dog. Her ability to navigate the demands of family, creativity, and professional growth allows her to connect authentically with others, sharing her insights with warmth and approachability.

Acknowledgements

I wish to thank, first of all, my family who have supported me over this incredible journey. Your curiosity, and certainty sustain me when I have very little for myself. Thank you, Tony, Leland, and Daphne, for believing in my story.

Thank you, Mom, for writing down my first stories to send as entertainment to Kimmy, my sister who encouraged me to tell my tales. And thank you to my sister Kay-Kay, for buying books that would fuel my world. Finally, to my brother, Bobby, thank you for buying me a Barbie Ferrari so that Ken could be Magnum, P.I.

For my friends who braved reading this book at its various stages, thank you. Your insights are more valuable than you will ever know, and your trust that it wouldn't ruin our friendship is most humbling. Thank you Amy Patton, Brandi Keplinger, Emily McGrann, Erica van Pelt, and Rachel Murawski.

To my "medical team" who helped me dream up ways to kill and save my darlings, I thank you for sharing your dark humor and years of schooling in the art of Medicine. Thank you Dianna Street, RN, BSN, Lillian Esker, RN, BSN, Benjamin Schumbrecht, DNP, APRN, and (by proxy) Dr. Matthew Schumbrecht.

Thank you to my professional editor, Amy Patton. Your tiny-ass handwriting has brought me joy for over thirty years. To Aarin Pound, thank you for your kind edits and suggestions.

Book Club

Discussion Questions

1. Claudia leaves town at the first chance she gets, seeking adventure, while Eleanor tries to build her life based on unwritten rules that have been given to her. However, real life is much more complex than following that one choice for the rest of your life. How, if at all, did the choices made by each sister relate to your own life? Did it evoke any memories or create any connections for you?

2. The focus of the book is on the two narrators: Claudia and Eleanor. But there are many interesting secondary characters in the lives of the sisters. How did they contribute to the story? Who was your favorite? Who was your least favorite?

3. How did the novel explore themes such as love, trust, communication, family, identity, or sexuality? How did the author balance the romance in the story with other elements such as humor, suspense, drama, or social commentary?

4. What were some of your favorite scenes from the book? Why did they stand out to you?

5. What was the most challenging part of the book for you to read or understand? How did you overcome it, if you did?

6.   Each sister has her romance in this story. Were the romance arcs believable to you? Why or why not? How did you feel about the chemistry between Claudia and Spencer? Do you think Eleanor and Nick are compatible? Are you rooting for the couples?

7.   The author brings some spice to the table; how did you like the heat in the novel?

8.   What do you think happens to the couples after the novel ends? Would you want to go back to River Styx for more?

9.   If Hollywood were casting the movie version of this book, who would you like to see in the various roles; Claudia, Eleanor, Diedre, Alice, Greg, Nick, Spencer, Patrick, etc.?

10. In Greek Mythology the River Styx is the border of the world of the living from the world of the dead, and is the first of five rivers a soul must pass to get to the Underworld. Drinking from the river Lethe caused a soul to forget. In some stories, the ferryman, Chiron, assists souls in crossing the river Acheron, the river of woe. While the town is named for the River Styx, each part of the book is named after one of the other rivers. Do you feel like the author met the definition of each river in each part of the book?

www.ingramcontent.com/pod-product-compliance
Lightning Source LLC
Chambersburg PA
CBHW071602110726
47908CB00007B/2212